Jeli

Condo for Sale
Dead man not included!

Bradley Farm Series
Book 4

MARY JANE FORBES

Todd Book Publications

JELI
Condo for Sale
Dead man not included!

ISBN: 978-0692720974 (sc)
Printed in the United States of America
Todd Book Publications: 5/30/2016
Port Orange, Florida

Author photo: Geri Rogers
Cover photo: Anna Jurkovska, Dreamstime.com
Cover design 2018 by Angie: pro_ebookcovers

Books by Mary Jane Forbes

Bradley Farm Series
Bradley Farm, Sadie, Finn
Jeli, Marshall, Georgie

The Baker Girl
One Summer, Promises

Twists of Fate Series
The Fisherman, a love story
The Witness, living a lie
Twists of Fate, daring to dream

Murder by Design, Series:
Murder by Design
Labeled in Seattle
Choices, And the Courage to Risk

Elizabeth Stitchway, PI, Series
The Mailbox, Black Magic,
The Painter, Twister

House of Beads Mystery Series
Murder in the House of Beads
Intercept, Checkmate
Identity Theft

Novels - standalone
The Baby Quilt … a mystery!
The Message…Call Me!

Short Stories
Once Upon a Christmas Eve, a Romantic Fairy Tale
The Christmas Angel and the Magic Holiday Tree

Visit: www.MaryJaneForbes.com

Bradley Family Tree

Marshall Bradley
1810-1880

Kenneth Bradley
1845-1920

Mason Bradley
1896-1946

Arnold Bradley
1927-1970

Daniel Bradley
1951-

Offspring—Jane and Danny Bradley

Twins
Sadie & Marshall
|
Finn
|
Jeli

Wolfe's son
Georgie

Jeli

Condo for Sale
Dead man not included!

Prologue

———

The Guardian, British national daily newspaper, 2015/2016 Chinese Stock Market Crash

———

The Chinese stock market crash began with their market bubble popping on June 12, 2015. A third of the value of A-shares on the Shanghai Stock Exchange was lost within one month of the event. By July 9, 2015, the Shanghai stock market had fallen 30% over three weeks as 1,400 companies, or more than half listed, filed for a trading halt in an attempt to prevent further losses.

After three stable weeks the Shanghai index fell again on August 24, 2015, by 8.48%, marking the largest fall since 2007.

The market meltdown set off a global rout.

Chapter 1

Day after Christmas
2015

IT WAS A SPECTACULAR DAY. A sun-sparking-off-ice-crystals-hanging-from-the-eves kind of day. Anjelica Jane Bradley, known to friends and family as Jeli, was prepared, ready for her break-out job interview in thirty minutes. Not an in-person-interview, but a GoToMeeting appointment by means of her computer's internet hookup. Her potential new boss would see a professional interior designer spiffed up in a new black jacket, hanging in her closet for the past three years, over a new white blouse. Jeans and pink kitten slippers bouncing on the floorboards —out of sight under her desk.

A great start to the day after Christmas.

Today it didn't matter that the months, years, leading to this hour were littered with four attempts at graduating with a college degree. Before striking out on her own, she had followed, one by one, the choices of her three older siblings—their paths to success, but not for her.

Her online-diploma came in the mail last week and at this very moment was standing by for the frame she snagged from the attic. The online course proved to be perfect, her final choice, fast-tracking her career in interior design. But the classes in architecture were in person—a bricks and mortar classroom, a professor who shook her hand. It didn't matter that her engagement to what's-his-name was broken ten months prior.

No, sirree! Today was a new beginning.

Humming, she fastened shiny new silver hoops to her ears, dabbed perfume on her wrist. Not only did she project a professional image to the other side of the screen, but a little of her favorite scent boosted her spirits on this side as well. Her cell phone's ringtone, a jazzy version of *When the Saints Go Marching In,* signaled an incoming call. Checking the caller ID, she smiled. It was the GoToMeeting man.

"Ms. Bradley?"

"Yes, this is Ms. Bradley. I'm very excited—"

"Yes, well, I'm sorry, but I have to cancel our appointment."

"Oh. When would you like to reschedule? I'm pretty flex—"

"I spoke with my partners, and we agree you aren't a good fit for our company...for our clients. The presentation you submitted was very nice, but you lack experience. Of course, you can contact us again...in a few years...if you pursue your career in design."

"Oh." Jeli slumped on her desk chair, the springs in her fiery red hair collapsing.

"Yes, I'm sorry. I had looked forward to meeting you. But I wish you success in the new year."

"Oh...sure."

The cell display faded.

The call disconnected.

"So much for a big break-out interview," she muttered with a heavy sigh. "Twenty resume packets, loaded with my designs. Eighteen rejections. Make that nineteen."

Lucas, a small dog with very curly, sugar-cookie colored fur, dashed into her room, making a flying leap for her bed. He missed. Tried again, nestling on the pillow. Lucas was Finn's dog. A stray her brother picked up abandoned on a highway. Finn was Jeli's senior by almost five years.

"You're right, Lucas. If at first you don't, blah, blah, blah. Can you believe it? Nineteen developers and not a one with the vision to see the potential in my designs. Gee willikers, my professors gave me all A's. I've had clients. They loved my designs."

Lucas gave a yelp, agreeing with her.

"That's right, Lucas. My three best, meticulous designs." Jeli turned to her dresser, snatched her brush to restore the springs in her shoulder-length red hair. "There was the seaside mansion in

Kennebunkport, Maine—my favorite. And I had raves for my work on the Boston condo, and the renovation of that Victorian townhouse in Newburyport. Sure, the condo was for my brother Marshall. But the two houses came from drop-ins at the farm's antique shop. Those three commissions totaled up to a year's tuition—not chump change. So they had to be good. Very good." She nodded at her reflection, giving another vicious swipe at her hair.

"Jeli, come on down. Lunch is ready," Jane called up the stairs. Her mom was serving a hot lunch on this very cold December day.

Tossing her head with a huff, Jeli headed for the stairs. "Come on, Lucas. Slap a smile on that muzzle. Show some teeth. No frowns for us."

Hustling down the two flights of stairs, Lucas at her heels, Jeli entered the kitchen, giving her mom and pop a hug.

"All set for the interview?" Jane asked.

"Temporary change in plans. I was ready but the developer canceled. Same old story…lack of experience."

"Umm, I'm sorry, dear. I know you were counting…looking forward to the prospect…" Jane didn't finish her thought. Better to leave her daughter's disappointment alone, knowing she always seemed to bounce back. She didn't miss a beat dishing up bowls of chili from the slow cooker as Pops pulled up Gran's chair to the head of the table. Her husband's mother, late eighties, never missed a meal with the family, even if there were just two or three, or a get-together with the whole clan. She didn't say much unless she was moved to drop one of her pearls of wisdom.

Danny, lovingly referred to as Pops, had concerns over his youngest, Anjelica Jane, wondering if she would ever settle into her calling, calling being the operative word. She was called in numerous directions. Easygoing on one hand, she was driven on the other. A creative dynamo, observant, missed nothing. Oh, yes, she could be flirtatious when she wanted to be. As the baby of the family, she learned early on that a little sugar got her what she wanted quicker than throwing a temper tantrum.

"What are you going to do now?" Gran asked, testing a spoon of chili for heat—heat from the cooker and the spices. She wasn't worried. Her sprightly granddaughter never let anything get her down. She swung from one thing to another—sure of herself, she never seemed to look back.

"Well, Gran, I still have one presentation packet out. It only takes one. Maybe I'll get lucky. My goal was to have a job before the end of the year—six more days. Mom, do you have a shamrock in your hanky drawer? It seems I need a dash of your Irish luck."

Chapter 2

New Year's Eve
2015

SOPPING-WET COTTON BALLS were falling from the sky. Jeli, nose pressed to her bedroom window atop the old farmhouse, each breath frosting the glass, assumed there were clouds above, but the flakes were so thick, she couldn't see them. Only thirteen more hours until the stroke of midnight, her goal of a job by the end of the year seemed doomed to failure. Would she live with her parents forever, not that it wasn't pleasant. But really, turning thirty-five today and still sleeping in her third-floor bedroom?

Five days had passed since the rejection of her job application. Now, it was the last day of the year and her frustration was mounting. Pacing in the privacy of her room, her mind flitted from one option to another. Should she place a call to the outstanding receiver of her job presentation? Or, should she wait it out, forget about him? He obviously wasn't interested. Why bother with him, if he didn't pay her the courtesy of saying, "thanks, but no thanks." Yes, that's what she would do—forget him, prepare twenty new, even more scintillating packets.

Decision made, she padded to the shower. Letting the hot water wash down the drain any doubts about her plan to move forward, her tiny bathroom filled with steam.

Stepping out of the shower, Jeli quickly wrapped her body in the white terry bathrobe, looped a towel around her dripping hair, and opened the bathroom door.

Removing the towel from her damp hair, she heard her computer ping—a new message. Bending over the desk chair, she grasped the mouse, clicked to open the email.

———

11:30 a.m.

J. Bradley, I received your resume with attached documents. My name is Josh Greely. I'm a developer. You answered my ad in the Boston Globe. I'd like to set up an interview, that is, if you haven't accepted another offer. Let me know if you're interested.

Josh Greely

———

"Well, would you look at that, missy? Mr. Greely is a discerning gentleman who obviously sees the potential in your designs." Letting the towel drop to the floor, Jeli slid onto the desk chair and clicked *Reply*.

11:36 a.m.

Mr. Greely, I haven't accepted another job offer yet...still in the process of deciding. I'd be happy to speak with you. When do you suggest?

J. Bradley

———

11:38 a.m.

How about now? You mentioned in your cover letter that you would be available for a preliminary chat using Skype on your computer?

Josh Greely

———

Jeli turned to the full-length mirror on her closet door. Drips of water puddling at her feet, tangled wet hair, body wrapped in terry cloth.

11:41 a.m.
I have an errand to run. Back in thirty minutes. Would that work for you?
J. Bradley

———

11: 43 a.m.
Make it an hour. One o'clock. Are you familiar with GoToMeeting?
Josh Greely

———

11:45 a.m.
Yes, very familiar.
J. Bradley

———

11:48 a.m.
Good. One o'clock then. I'll set it up, send you the login information.
Josh Greely

———

11:50 a.m.
I look forward to it, Mr. Greely.
J. Bradley

———

With a fist pump, Jeli glanced sideways at the closet mirror, smiled at her reflection, then made a dash for the hair dryer.

"Jeli, Gran and I are having a cup of coffee. Can you join us?" Jane called from the bottom of the staircases.

"Can't, Mom. Any chance you could bring me a cup? I have an interview in less than an hour."

Making quick work with the hair drier, smoothing the red corkscrew curls to a gentle curve, she kissed her mom's cheek as she set a cup of hot coffee on the bathroom counter.

"Good luck, sweetie," Jane said, making a fast retreat.

There was no time to fuss with the back of her hair. Mr. Greely wouldn't see it anyway. With quick steps to her dresser, Jeli attached the silver hoops, worn once, casting a twinkle of light. Dashing to the closet, she snatched her interview clothes—the worn-once white blouse, and definitely the black blazer, again— just right, sophisticated and professional.

Glancing in her closet to see if there was anything else to add, she caught sight of the wallpaper scattered with wild flowers. Flowers droopy minutes before, their stems were now plucky with renewed vigor.

Dressed, she pulled a folder from the desk drawer, boosted up on her bed and thumbed through her designs preparing for any questions Mr. Greely might throw at her.

She looked up hearing her computer ping, alerting another message had arrived. Sliding onto her desk chair, finger on the mouse, she opened the message. Positioning the headset with microphone, she read the login instructions to the meeting with Mr. Greely.

Checking the webcam atop her monitor, Jeli squared her shoulders and logged into the GoToMeeting internet room with a bright smile on her face—not too broad, just right.

The fluffy pink kitten slippers on her feet were bouncing up and down under her daisy covered pajama bottoms.

Suddenly, his image filled the screen in front of her, Mr. Josh Greely. Her brows hitched up over her emerald green eyes. A very handsome man was looking back at her—short blonde hair curled around his ears, a black tie with a perfect Windsor knot at the neck of a starched white collar.

———

JOSH PEERED AT THE pretty face framed in his computer's monitor.

"Who are you? I have a meeting set up with J. Bradley," he said.

The face giggled. "I'm J. Bradley. Actually, Anjelica Jane Bradley, but I go by my nickname, Jeli."

"Excuse me. I was looking for a male interior designer—"

"See...that's why I sign all my correspondence with J. Now, unless you're going to hold my sex against me, discrimination is very bad you know, let's chat about my credentials."

The face, her face didn't look too friendly—a definite scowl over a defiant chin.

"Okay, Miss Anjelica—"

"That would be Ms. Anjelica J. Bradley. You can call me Jay, or Bradley, if that makes you feel better, seeing how you wanted a male designer. Now, tell me about the job. I've been designing for years so you're speaking with someone who knows her profession."

Years? She didn't look that old. Josh knew how women looked at different ages. He had four sisters—two older, two younger. So this Bradley person wasn't putting anything over on him. He had to be careful who he hired as a designer—knowledgeable and tough. There was a lot riding on it.

Bradley seemed to have an edge to her...could be useful, push back on vendors so they don't overcharge. Josh was determined to show his father, Joshua Greely Senior, that he, Joshua Greely Junior, could make it on his own as a contractor and now a developer. He had scraped enough funds together to buy a rundown brownstone in a rundown neighborhood located in the outer fringe of Boston, a forgotten neighborhood. Developers who had already turned a profit in the core of the city had no appetite to tackle another decrepit neighborhood. "Been there, done that," they said.

But it was a hard business to break into. Josh Greely was on the bottom rung of the local developer ladder, clawing his way to the top. He saw the row of forgotten brownstones as perfect for his meager resources, almost depleting the trust fund his grandfather set up for him. Because the whole street was rundown, the owner was anxious to dump the property enabling Josh to swing the deal.

"How can you have years of experience? I checked—you just received your degree."

"I have years of experience in interior design, overseeing renovations for men and women buying old, excuse me, make that antique homes in northern Massachusetts and in New Hampshire and Maine. You see, they came to Bradley Farm Antiques for furnishings and, well, I took it from there. I had absolutely no time to get a degree…until now. Did you even look at the video clip, and the PowerPoint presentation I sent you—all the pictures showing my design expertise?"

"Yes, I did."

The heels of Josh's bare feet were beating the floor. He loosened his tie, unbuttoned the collar of his shirt sliding over his jockey shorts. He began to sweat.

What should he do?

The face, the pretty face, waves of very red hair…*call her bluff*.

"Okay, Miss Bradley. Excuse me, Ms. Bradley, I'm in a bit of time crunch. Can you meet me tomorrow so I can show you the property? We'll talk."

"Tonight's New Year's Eve. I'm going to a party. Are you sure you'll be up for a meeting New Year's Day?"

Crap, he forgot. "I know that. It's just that I have so many appointments…"

Her face immediately changed—plump red lips spreading into a smile.

"Tomorrow is fine. Take a look at your building. Then we can have coffee and discuss things," she said.

Of course she's going to a party. New Year's Eve, pretty girl. Well, he was going to hang out with his folks, his sisters. It wasn't as if he had *nothing* to do.

"Okay then. Tomorrow it is." Josh scrunched his brows. He'd have to give his father an excuse for leaving before the football games started. He certainly wasn't going to let on what he was doing—buying the brownstone, hiring a designer...*maybe* hiring a designer.

Everything was riding on breaking up the brownstone into condos, selling each at a high price so he could immediately turn it over, buying the buildings on either side. He needed a brilliant, cheap designer with some knowledge of architecture, the bones of a building—load-bearing walls, experience blowing out walls for an open concept without the floor above caving in.

"What time? Where..." The plump lips spoke, paused, waiting for his answer.

Josh had no choice. All the other applicants laughed at what he offered to pay for their work. Ms. Bradley seemed hungry, had spunk. "Noon. Take the train to South Station...I'll send you directions, the address. Call Uber taxi service—they always have a driver available. We'll meet at the property—ring the bell."

The GoToMeeting webpage evaporated, leaving Jeli's desktop with a picture of Lucas front and center. A quick jog around her bed, head high like a majorette, she was sure she had a job. And, glory-be, with ten hours to spare before the new year.

Chapter 3

———

BECAUSE OF A PENDING snowstorm, the Bradley family had trekked early from points south and east to the family farm in Lakeville, New Hampshire, for the birthday celebration of the last sibling, Anjelica Jane.

The farmhouse hosted many affairs but New Year's Eve was always special. This New Year's Eve Jeli would share her birthday spotlight with the newlyweds, Finn and Kate along with Daisy, Kate's niece. The couple married over the Christmas holiday in Cinderella's Castle, Disney World. Daisy was the flower girl and bridesmaid rolled into one.

Finn's business partner, Cameron Foster and his wife Carrie, greeted the new Bradley couple in the barn where the two couples toiled in preparation to open a brewpub in March. Finn and Kate wasted no time or money in Cinderella's castle—two days—returning to the task of completing the renovation of the barn. A honeymoon would have to wait.

The pub space was the scene of a family gathering on Christmas eve, so tables and chairs were already setup on the restored oak floorboards providing a warm backdrop for tonight's celebration, a new year that held promise of big changes at Bradley Farm and the members of the Bradley clan.

Yesterday, Marshall picked up Sadie and Travis, flying in from Washington D.C., at Boston's Logan Airport. Their arrival at the farm propelled the celebration into high gear.

First up on the celebration agenda, Jeli's launch into an exciting new career.

The soon-to-be brewpub glittered with candles ensconced in glass hurricane shades down the center of a string of pine harvest tables. Tonight was her thirty-fifth birthday and her big sister and brother, first-born twins, were not going to let the baby of the family forget that it was her SPECIAL day.

———

THE FARMHOUSE WAS BUILT in 1840 by Marshall Bradley, the patriarch of the clan. The current Bradley, number five, married a winsome Irish lass, Jane O'Neill. Daniel Bradley, Jane's husband, was affectionately called Pops. His mother, Martha, was known by all as Gran. While the family chattered, laughed, poking fun at each other, Gran experienced twinges of sadness in her eyes that Arnie, her late husband never knew his grandchildren.

Tonight seemed right with the world, especially with the youngest managing to nail down an interview in Boston tomorrow. Everyone called her Jeli since her brother Finn couldn't manage Anjelica always saying Jeli. She had made a run at other career paths trying to follow in the footsteps of her twin siblings, Sadie and Marshall. Twins conceived on their parent's wedding night. Jeli spent a year as a student in computer science like her brother Marshall, an over-the-top cyber security programmer, who now had his own start-up business in Boston. But she found writing computer code daunting and so moved on, spending a year as a rookie reporter like her sister Sadie. Finally she trusted her instincts, trying something that had been in her mind all along—interior design with a minor in architecture.

Each sibling's footprint had pinched but the last one fit like Cinderella's glass slipper—hopefully. She had a good eye for space, coupled with the ability to bring together emotion and functionality using color, fabric, wood and tile.

Now, another New Year's Eve and another family celebration.

Jane smiled at her husband seated at the other end of the line of harvest tables. They loved having the family together, always accompanied with lively chatter, laughter, slinging barbs at each other, tonight mostly aimed at Jeli. Her eyes circled around her cherished family, feeling Wolfe's eyes on her, she nodded. She couldn't help thinking what a miracle it was that Wolfe and his son Georgie became part of their family. She'd never forget the day when Wolfe walked up the driveway of Bradley Farm carrying Georgie, a four-month-old baby in a basket, asking if she could spare some milk. Not as a gift, oh no, he'd work for the milk, maybe a meal for himself.

Jane turned her attention to Finn's new partners in the brewpub—Cameron and Carrie Foster. They were such a happy couple and good workers. Finn was a new man after he met the Fosters, and especially after they found they had dreams of a brewery in common. The Fosters moved from Colorado, and now lived on the farm in their tiny house parked by the lake on the back of the property, next to the tree house where Wolfe and Georgie lived. And then Finn and Katie parked their tiny house a few yards from the Fosters.

A chorus of the birthday song interrupted Jane's thoughts as Sadie emerged from the brewpub's unfinished kitchen carrying a cake blazing with thirty-five candles.

"Okay, Jeli-bean, let's see if you can blow them out this year," Finn said with a smirk.

Jeli shot him a sideways glare. "You just watch me, brother dear. You haven't blown yours out lately, umm, that would be forty if my memory serves me." She relaxed, basking in their celebration of her birthday and with the knowledge of her interview tomorrow in Boston with Mr. Josh Greely. *Let's see, Boston is an hour away. Shouldn't be much traffic on the first day of the year.* Sucking in a deep breath, she blew out all thirty-five candles, beaming at the applause and wishes for a happy new year.

Finn, and Georgie jumped to their feet, each snatching a champagne bottle from a tub of ice, snuggled against additional bottles. Champagne corks popped, and with Marshall's help holding up the glasses, the boys poured the bubbly. Jane locked eyes with Danny—yes, the farm was alive, well, and growing with activity.

Clinking glasses, chants of Happy New Year, hugging and kissing ensued. Jeli stepped behind her mom and pop and Gran, giving each a squeeze. "I'm so lucky to be part of this family. I love you."

Gran leaned back, a grin spreading across her face. It was going to be a good new year. She could feel it in her almost ninety-year-old bones.

Chapter 4

———

New Year's Day
2016

JELI OPTED TO FOLLOW Marshall into Boston rather than take the T. Living in Boston for several years, he knew his way around the city and had a good idea where the brownstone was located from the address Josh Greely had emailed to her as promised. Luckily she found a parking spot a few doors down the street, waving to Marshall as his black Jeep passed.

Grabbing her tote and laptop, she slid out of her slightly dinged silver coupe. Shading her eyes from the brilliant sun striking mounds of snow piled up at the curb, she gazed up at the four-story brownstones lining the street, the red brick sidewalks, street lamps and trees miraculously poking up through the bricks along with the weeds. She visualized an amazing spring when the trees burst into leaf. The street looked like it had been plucked from Boston's Back Bay where many such buildings were constructed in the mid 1800s. Most had been renovated but these buildings looked like they were ready for the wrecking ball.

Jeli mounted the cracked brick steps to a green door with two small frosted window panes. The paint was chipped and a brass kick plate tarnished black. She pushed button 4A.

A male voice immediately squawked from the speaker beside the row of buttons. "Hello, Can I help you?"

"J. Bradley to see Mr. Josh Greely. I have a one o'clock appointment."

"Ah, good. When you hear the buzzer, the door will release. Step in. At the end of a short hall you'll see an elevator. I'll meet you there."

"Gee, at least he sounded like he was expecting me," she murmured.

At the buzzer Jeli pushed the door open, stepping into a small vestibule and hallway. Mailboxes lined the wall to the right. Bare light bulbs hung from the ceiling providing a shadowy glow. The scent of lemon oil on old wood was reminiscent of the treatment her mom used on the antiques in her shop to preserve their luster. However, the lemon scent was the only trace of preservation as it mixed with a musty smell of an abandoned building.

Hesitating, she spotted the elevator at the same time the door slid open. The man stepping out was the man she had seen on the webcam yesterday. Make that the same good-looking guy. A smile crossed her face as she quickly walked down the hall. She stuck out her hand grasping his extended in greeting. "Well, Ms. Bradley, I thought you were kidding me, maybe posing as a male family member yesterday."

Taking her hand, he turned it over examining it.

"Excuse me. What's with my hand? Part of the interview?"

"No, no, I was surprised. You have a strong grip. Your skin is smooth but not that soft. Bradley Farm. Do you drive a tractor? Lift bales of hay?"

"I have been known to perform both tasks, but with two brothers I've learned to protect myself. However, I do schlep furniture around, antiques, with my mom."

"I see. Well, let's go up...fourth floor, I'll show you the space."

Riding up the elevator, Jeli glanced at Mr. Greely out of the corner of her eyes. She was five foot five, and he was more than a head taller. He looked to be muscular under his black turtleneck sweater. Probably as a contractor he schlepped stuff around the same as she. A tingle shot down her spine as his light cologne circled her nose. Yup, Mr. Greely was tall, fair skinned, and way too handsome to be riding in an elevator small enough to bump elbows.

With a thump the elevator stopped, the door slid to the right revealing a construction site—studs formed the outline of rooms on the right, and rustic brick walls to the left.

Through the framing Jeli could see windows marching around the space, new glass framed by sanded oak, ready to be finished. Stepping from the elevator she walked through the framed doorway, strode to the bay window with a view of the trees and the street below. Turning, she faced Josh Greely standing, arms crossed, watching her.

"What do you think?" he asked.

Pulling her tan car coat tighter against the cold musty air, she was right in wearing her black wool slacks. From what little he said on the phone, she expected the building would be empty, hence no heat.

"I think this space is going to be spectacular. The location of the building is ripe to be returned to its former grandeur. Explain the floor plan. It looks airy—"

Greely laughed. "Well sure, it's only studding—"

Her brows shot up. "Duh! I assume you're keeping the space open? Living room, dining room?" Jeli stepped through a doorway, her eyes darting around.

"Come on. Let's go to the unit that has walls, then we'll go for coffee." He led the way to the right of the elevator, opening the door to a mirror layout of the opposite side, with the exception of being only one bedroom.

"If you counted the floors when you parked, you saw that the building is four stories, plus a basement level, with high windows looking out above the sidewalk to the street. My plan is to maximize the space and hopefully my investment. Two condos on each floor, a two bedroom, and a one bedroom, nice size bathroom, small powder room, the rest open—kitchen to dining room to large living room. Each condo will feature the original bay window in the front. I want to keep the lines clean, uncluttered."

"Nice. Do you have buyers lined up?"

"A few are interested. I have a couple of realtors who are monitoring the space as it develops. The idea is that it would be for a couple without children, bachelors, bachelorettes looking for a place in the city. There's a T-stop...a couple of short blocks."

"And you called me because?" Jeli turned from the bay window, walked to the opposite end. Her mind was galloping with one design dissolving into another. She loved the space. Compact, yet open. Five levels, two condos each, ten units total. A dream job, and throw in tall, fair, and handsome..."

"I called because I'm looking for a designer who understands the bones of a building, the architectural plusses and restraints, to bring this one to life, as a model showcasing the potential of the units. To keep tabs on the construction, the renovation, I'm going to live in this one ... temporarily."

"Where do you live now?"

When he didn't answer, she glanced at him over her shoulder. *Too personal a question?*

Jeli twisted around taking in the space adjacent to the one she first viewed. Plumbing sprouted from the wall where the open kitchen was located. Stepping through the doorway to the bathroom, the plumbing for the bathroom fixtures appeared to be ready. "When are you planning to move in? There's still a lot—"

"Two weeks. At least be able to camp out until everything is in place. Three weeks, worst case four weeks. A buyer is going to be in the city at the end of January. I want to have the two units ready to show him."

"And... what..." Her words trailed off. Mr. Josh Greely was out of his mind. No way can he have this space ready to show—

"So, can you help me?"

"What exactly are you looking for from me—lighting, plumbing, flooring—colors, materials..." She trailed off, arms swinging from ceiling to floor, pointing at the pipes hanging from the walls. "Furniture?"

"Yes, all of that, Ms. Bradley."

What ... all of that? "Whew," a puff of air escaped her plump rouged lips. "Knock off the Ms. Bradley. Call me—"

"It'll be Ms. Bradley if we're with a client, otherwise...I'll call you Red." Josh began to pace, right fist punching his left palm.

"Look, Red, I'll be honest with you. I've talked to several designers …they all want…I couldn't afford them. I know you're new, starting out, in spite of what you said on the phone yesterday. But I really liked your presentation—the pictures—the rooms were your work?"

Okay, layout it for him. "Yes. As long as we're being honest, they were quick designs for clients who continually buy antiques from my mom's antique shop on the farm, and the contemporary sleek rooms were for my brother's condo, a pricey area. He stretched his budget and bought a space needing renovation, in bad shape like yours."

"Well, I liked them. Each had a quality…a touch of home. They didn't come across glossy, cold. I think my potential buyer—"

"This buyer, what does he want? Did he give you some ideas of what he's looking for—married, single—"

"Well, see, there's a bit of a language barrier. But—"

"Where's he from?" Jeli asked.

"China."

"Chinese?"

"Yes." Josh sighed.

The image of cherry and pine Early American, or mahogany and walnut Victorian antiques dissolved. Jeli turned to the bay window. *Chinese? Think, missy. Think.* "Oh, you mean like bright colors—green, blue, yellow, and of course, red. Chinese love red. It's considered the luckiest of all colors in China."

How lame can I get, she thought. Colors are only the beginning. I need a crash course on Chinese culture or I'm sure to design something offensive. Maybe I should turn down this job. Turn it down? No way. It's the only offer I have. It's day one of a new year, of my goal. A cup of strong coffee is what I need—rev up the creative adrenalin.

"Let's get a coffee," Josh said. "Put together a game plan."

"My thought exactly."

Chapter 5

———

A BRISK JANUARY WIND kicked up over Boston. Jeli noted that Josh didn't seem to notice, jabbing his fists into his parka's pockets. She pulled up the collar of her wool car coat wishing she had worn her parka. She tied her long purple scarf tighter around her neck, the ends catching in the breeze as they scurried the two blocks to a coffee shop. The plate-glass windows of the small intimate café were steamy from the warm air inside and frigid air outside. Josh opened the door, stepped inside, and strode to a corner table.

Expecting a gentleman, Jeli was almost hit in the face by the door swinging shut. Okay, so Mr. Handsome has no manners. Let it go, Jeli. Mr. Handsome does have a job opening. An incredibly challenging job opening, so buck up. You're not a girl, you're a designer.

"Happy New Year, Josh. Didn't expect you today," Millie said, grinning at the girl sliding onto the chair next to her regular customer.

"Thank God you're open. It's freezing out there," Josh said, rubbing his hands together.

"The owner always opens after New Year's Eve. Figures the neighborhood needs to sober up. What can I get you? Your usual?"

"Two please, Millie. Large."

Jeli took off her mittens, blew into her palms to warm her nose. "I think we're in for an ice storm tonight don't you?"

Josh ignored her question, pulling a small notepad from his pocket, along with a ballpoint pen. Holding the cap between his teeth, he began making notes.

Jeli followed suit but with her new smart phone, a present from Pops. A Samsung. Someday she'd spring to join the Apple ecosystem.

Millie set the coffees on the table, then hustled off to pour refills for the customers at the counter.

Taking a sip, Jeli squinted at Josh over the rim. "Did you mean it? Three weeks to be ready for your client—an open house with furniture, drapes—"

"I always mean what I say. And I want to plan on two weeks. Always shoot for the best possible time, Red."

Josh glanced at her hand, her ring finger. "You're not married?"

"If I was a male designer, would you have asked?"

He smiled, looked her in the eye. "Touché. No, I wouldn't have."

"Are you married, Mr. Greely?"

"No. No time. Now, tell me when I can see your ideas for the space. I have a contractor arriving tomorrow with his crew. The demolition is done unless they find something they didn't catch when they gutted the place. As you saw, the plumbing has been updated, just waiting for your suggestions on fixtures."

Jeli was ready. Walking to the coffee shop she had formulated a plan of attack. "Day after tomorrow I'll have preliminary sketches—lighting, flooring, paint colors, kitchen layout. Tomorrow your contractors can finish the studding, put up the drywall. I suggest you not close-in the kitchen. Keep it open— more light, a better flow with a dining-table area, and living room. Instead of a wall I propose a kitchen island, stools tucked under on the living room side. It will make a nice breakfast bar, or paperwork area for the new owner. Better use of the space. I brought my laser ruler for rough measurements. A floor plan would be helpful. What do you think?"

"I like it, Red. Yes, I have a floor plan. A file. Let me know if you can't open it."

"I work with SmartDraw for my projects," Jeli said. If your file doesn't work with—"

"I hear you. I use that program, so you won't have any trouble. Actually, it's great because we can update each other's drawings. I'm penny pinching too. Big plans, skinny budget, basically no funds. The day after tomorrow is a Sunday. The contractor may be working tomorrow, but I'm not paying him overtime for Sunday. So, we'll have plenty of time to go over your ideas."

"I want to go back to the building, check the space again. See if there are any details, like moldings, that we should keep, try to retain the character. Of course, with the demo already done, there won't be much left...but for the next project...that is, if you you're satisfied with my work. Which brings me to the question of pay?"

"What about it?"

"How much...you know, for my work? I don't consider you a charity case."

Josh looked out the window, feet twitching under the table. "Five hundred a week with a bonus if the property sells quickly. Understand, it's week to week. Now, Red, let's go back. There are a couple of things I have to check out, too. As for the next project...too early to tell."

"Does your Chinaman come with an interpreter?"

"The realtor I'm working with is from Shanghai. She only handles Chinese buyers who want real estate in the U.S. Most ask for New York City, but, more often than not, she persuades them to look at the Boston area. She speaks Mandarin as well as English."

"I've heard about some Chinese moving their money out of China. The Yuan continues to be devalued. Same for the Greeks."

"Opportunities, Ms. Bradley. Lots of opportunities—today the Chinese, tomorrow the Greeks."

The hair on Jeli's arm was on fire hearing Josh talk—all his ideas, and she was getting in on the ground floor. "Is 9:30 too early, Sunday?"

"9:30 it is. I'll have a thermos of coffee for us."

———

EXHILARATED, EXHAUSTED, Jeli's brain full of ideas vying for attention as she left Josh for the day at the condo, she slid into her car, throwing her tote on the passenger seat. Turning the key in the ignition, she let the motor idle to warm up. Her mind was a jumble. Opportunities Josh said. That was an understatement. And why on earth did she say she'd have preliminary sketches in two days? Leaning over, she fished around in the tote for her phone, punched #2.

"Marsh, I need—"

"Hey, little one, how did the interview go?"

"Oh, you won't believe it. I got the job, it's huge. It's a breakout opportunity...I'm in way over my head. Excited and scared. Can I stay with you for a couple of weeks? I have no time to prepare my presentation for the space and even less if I have to travel back and forth to the farm. I'm heading home to get my computer and stuff. Actually, I'm still parked where you left me—"

"Jeli, hold on. Stay where you are. I'll come to you. You can follow me back to the farm. We'll have dinner with the family so you can fill us all in, then leave your car home, and I'll drive you back to my place. You can crash as long as you like. Anyway, I promised Sadie and Travis I'd drive them to the airport tonight. How does that sound?"

"Like a lifeline."

Chapter 6

———

A LIGHT SNOW BEGAN to fall as the family rose from the dinner table. Sadie was surprised that Jeli didn't talk about her new boss, her new job, new responsibilities. Maybe on the drive to the airport she would be able to pry more out of her baby sister.

Running on fumes, Jeli scampered to her room to pack her computer equipment, and enough clothes to see her through a couple of weeks. She could always make a trip home on the train to fill in the gaps of her wardrobe if needed.

"Georgie, are you in the kitchen," Jeli called from the third floor landing.

"Sure am. Need something?"

"Please a flashlight and your help finding a big suitcase in the attic. Can you come up?"

"Be right with you."

Georgie mounted the stairs with the beam from the flashlight under his chin, a ghoulish grin crossing his face. Jeli shook her head. She wasn't in the mood.

"Hey, what's the matter? You've had a fantastic day—"

"Just tired. I hope I'm doing the right thing…the job, staying with Marsh."

"Trash talk. Not the Jeli I know—fearless, a creative dynamo. Come on, let's get that suitcase."

Jeli turned, led the way over the creaky floorboards to the unfinished attic adjacent to her room.

Opening the squeaky door, Georgie handed her another flashlight he picked up. The two of them flashed beams of light around the shadows.

"I remember when this was full to overflowing with furniture and boxes. So much has been sold in Mom's antique shop. Sorry, I guess I could have found the suitcase by myself," Jeli said.

"Always good to have another pair of hands. You may see something else you can use."

"Georgie, look at this cute case." Jeli picked it up to show him.

"Looks like an old train case the ladies used to carry when they traveled. You could put your hair stuff, cosmetics in it—out of Marshall's way. Is it empty?"

Jeli jiggled the case. "No, I hear something." She knelt on the old floorboards, her fingers tightening on the latch. Rubbing her arm as a brush of air tickled the hairs, she opened the lid. Georgie rubbed his arm as well. "Georgie, did you feel that...you rubbed your arm?"

"Did I? Reflexes I guess."

Their heads turned hearing a noise behind them.

"A ghost?" Jeli whispered.

"Maybe," Georgie said. "When I was hauling some of the furniture from here to the barn's antique shop, I'd hear things."

"Things? Like what?" Jeli asked, waving the flashlight slowly from wall to wall.

"A sigh...a female sigh, a whiff of perfume, or just an active imagination. What's in the case?"

"Looks like several pieces wrapped in tissue paper. Oh, how pretty. Georgie look, an antique mirror, like for a woman's dresser." Jeli quickly unwrapped the other items. "It's a dresser set—green marbleized Bakelite. Mom sold something similar in the shop but not nearly as beautiful as this. Two brushes, a comb and...a pin box. There's a slip of paper in the pin box...*Rosemary*."

"Jeli, there've been several items found with the name of Rosemary...different places on the farm. Remember when Finn and I cleaned out the barn for his brewery, he found a hymnal with her name in it. I think there was an inscription...*God Speed*."

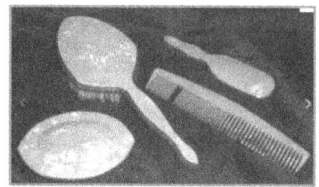

They both felt another brush of air, their hands touching their cheeks. "Rosemary, are you here?" Jeli whispered, her hand again lifting to her cheek. "Georgie, she kissed me...I swear, Rosemary kissed my cheek. I'm not afraid, are you?"

"No, she seems to be a friend. I've been on the lookout around the farm as I clean out a shed, a barn, taking furniture to your pops to refinish. I think Rosemary wants you and I to be her friend. This is the first time I've felt her presence. Of course, we can't tell the family. They'll think we've gone bonkers."

"She'll be our secret, Georgie. I'm going to take the brush and the comb with me. Maybe Rosemary will bring me luck."

"...at least watch over you...keep you safe."

―――――

WITH MUCH CHATTER, hugs and kisses, Marshall and Travis loaded the back of the jeep with suitcases, Jeli with the travel case between her feet in the backseat with Sadie. Rolling down the driveway they waved out the window to the family huddled at the back door of the farmhouse. Marshall turned east heading for Interstate 95. First stop, Logan Airport.

Marshall kept his eyes on the snow covered road. Travis was co-pilot watching for icy spots missed by the trucks moving in a conga line, spewing sand out the back.

Sadie turned to Jeli, patting her arm. "What do you think of your new boss? All you told us at dinner was that he was handsome and had big ideas. What's he really like?"

Jeli grasped her sister's hand. "He lacks manners, but I can give him a pass because when the café door almost hit me in the face, he wasn't thinking of me, but all that had to be accomplished in the next few weeks. He made it very clear he wasn't thrilled with me. He thought I was a male designer...he didn't want a female. But I think he was being honest when he said the designers he had interviewed turned him down because he was paying next to nothing."

"What was his offer?"

"Five hundred a week with a bonus if the property sold quickly, but...a big but, I might not last past the first week."

"He's getting a heck of deal. You could be out of a job in a week...on a whim."

"I know, but, Sadie, it could also be an incredible opportunity for me. I have to make it work...it's also very exciting. He has a client, from China, coming to see the space by the end of January—staged with furniture. I guess the man is prequalified. Mr. Greely is working with a Boston realtor who only deals with Chinese prospects, people who want to invest in the States."

"I hear Chinese investors are a booming market in Boston and New York City. Do you trust this Mr. Greely?" Marshall said over his shoulder.

"I don't really know anything about him." Jeli leaned forward against her seat belt, tapped Travis on the shoulder. "Travis, can you check out my new boss? See if he's legit. I didn't think of it until Marsh and I were driving to the farm."

"I'll give it a try. What's his full name? Live in Boston? Age? Description, other than handsome," he said with a chuckle.

"Josh Greely, developer...I didn't get a business card. Come to think of it, I don't even have his cell number. I do have his email address. I'll forward his first message to me once I get to Marsh's. I'd say he's in his thirties, almost six foot."

Jeli laid her hand on her brother's shoulder. "Marsh, do you have a Chinese girlfriend, or employee, acquaintance?"

"Girlfriend, no. Employee, yes. A programmer, Susan Li. She's been in the U. S. five years, if I remember right. Her family lives in Beijing. Susan came to the U.S. on a student visa...went to MIT, majored in computer science. Smart as whip. She's in the process of applying for citizenship...a long process. Several years."

"I want to meet her. I presume she speaks English?"

"Yes, and Mandarin. Jeli, I hope you'll be okay on the futon in the living room. I seem to recall, when you worked your interior design magic on my condo, you commented a futon was perfect for the occasional guest."

"It is perfect. Okay if I commandeer the entryway closet?"

"It's yours. I don't use it. When do you meet with Greely again?"

"Sunday morning, nine-thirty. I promised sketches with my ideas for the space—color palette and pictures of furniture for the staging to show his client."

"Yikes. Good thing I bought an extra supply of K-cups for the coffee maker you said *I had to have*. Airport ahead. What airline, Travis?"

"U.S. Air to Reagan—a hop, skip and a jump to our apartment," Sadie said.

"*Our apartment*...sounds very married. When are you two going to tie the knot?" Marshall asked.

"We're talking about summer...on the farm," Travis replied.

The sisters in the backseat exchanged broad smiles. With a sigh, Jeli pressed Sadie's hand to her lips.

"Hey, Jeli, what's with the Eskimo gear you picked up at the house—parka, boots? Planning on heading to Alaska and the Iditarod dog race?" Travis said.

"Well, Josh heads off down the street without a thought that I may not be able to keep up. This job isn't about looking good. It's a matter of survival, a dog-eat-dog world. I have to produce." Pausing, she giggled. "Of course, it never hurts to show a little leg, if I ever get out of these flannel-lined snow pants."

Chapter 7

———

TOSSING, TOSSING, TOSSING. Legs tangled, fighting the blanket.

Jeli bolted upright.

It was 3:05 a.m.

Sleep was impossible. Thoughts of the mysterious Josh Greely mingled with designs for his property, mixing with mounting apprehension over the looming deadline. She knew nothing about Chinese culture. A Chinese girl was in one of her architecture classes at the University of New Hampshire. They had lunch a couple of times. The girl was chatty, friendly. Jeli liked her but that was it. "From now on, I'm going to pay more attention to everyone I meet, ask questions, find out what makes them tick, even if it's just over an egg-salad sandwich!"

With the proclamation, she freed her legs from the blanket, grabbed her brother's bathrobe, and padded to the galley kitchen to brew a cup of coffee, a singleton. With the coffeemaker gurgling, she turned to the only table in Marshall's sparsely furnished condo. She gazed around what Marshall called home, thinking she should have pressed him harder to buy a few accessories, but he liked the sleek uncluttered look. It was small, one bedroom, but he owned the wicked view of the city.

She fired up her computer, picked up a cup of piping hot coffee, and set to work.

At six o'clock she heard Marshall approach on bare feet behind her.

"You've been busy," he said picking up a yellow tablet, several pages turned back, all filled with notes.

"I couldn't sleep. Marsh, do you think I could meet the woman you spoke of last night? I believe you said her name is Susan Li?"

"It's a little early to call her, but I'll send her a text. After a shower, I'm heading in to work. If she hasn't replied, I'll probably see her there. She spends as much time as I do at work, so she might be happy to break for lunch, unless she has plans. After all, it's still a holiday weekend, sis."

"The more I Google for information about Chinese customs, culture, what they like in their home, the more questions I have. If Susan can't make it for lunch, maybe a cup of coffee. I need some direction...that is if she's willing."

Marshall picked up his cell from the counter, tapped a message, and headed to the bathroom.

Jeli dug around the bottom cabinet and pulled out a Mr. Coffee. There were times a pot was required over a singleton. That done she poked around the fridge to see what she could find for breakfast. She was starving.

By the time Marshall returned, scrambled eggs, bagels with cream cheese, and fresh coffee filled his condo with the aroma of breakfast food. As he fixed his plate with the eggs and a bagel, he checked his cell. "Susan said she can make it for coffee. Asks if nine-thirty is good for us. Okay with you?" he asked as he sat down at the other end of the table.

"Wonderful. Tell her, yes."

"I'll just introduce you, then be on my way, so you two can get acquainted. There's a café down the street from my company...I think I met you there for lunch once—"

"I remember. This condo was good buy, Marsh. Handy to your work, only a few blocks from the park, the theatre district. After we selected your furniture, I never really thought about your life...away from the farm."

"Umm...of course, but the decorator put the cherry on the top. Dress warm, Jeli-bean. It's a bit blustery out today."

"Not a problem. I'm all set—car coat or parka, black turtleneck, jeans. Oh, and my purple scarf. I learned from my visit with Josh Greely to dress warmly—marching from the property to the café for coffee and back."

———

JELI HIKED TO THE café early. She wanted to prioritize her questions. She had no idea how much time Susan was going to be able to spend with her. One thing she knew for sure, it was going to be an all-nighter putting together preliminary plans—layouts, colors, furnishings for Josh's property. She planned to give him some ideas for the adjacent space as well, being he was going to live there temporarily. *I wonder where he plans to live after that. Never asked. Does he have family nearby?*

The bell on the café door jingled as Marshall held it open for a stunning woman. Her shiny, coal black hair was straight to just below her shoulders, feathered in front under her chin. The petite woman was dressed in all black—wool thigh-length cape belted in front through side slits allowing the back to flow freely over leggings into high-heeled boots. The only color a red cashmere scarf looped around her neck.

Marshall pointed her to one of the two booths in the back.

Jeli, feeling like a hippo in her bulky outerwear, closed her laptop and slid out of the booth, her hand extended.

"Susan, this is my sister, Anjelica. We call her Jeli. And Jeli, this is Susan Li." Marshal nodded to Susan.

"Susan, it's a pleasure to meet you...such short notice...thanks," Jeli said shaking Susan's hand.

"The pleasure is mine. Marshall told me a little about your project. Sounds very ambitious." Susan removed her cape, hung it on the peg, and slid into the booth opposite Jeli.

"I'll leave you girls to your discussions. Have fun." Marshall smiled, hunching down in his quilted jacket and left.

Jeli took note of Susan's eyes following him out of the café, the door swinging shut after him. She thought she caught something in the look but promptly forgot as she turned her focus to Susan.

"Marsh says you've lived in Boston several years?" Jeli said, smiling.

"Yes. I went to school at MIT and now I'm a programmer in a very exciting start-up, your brother's company."

"Your parents are still in China?"

"They flew over from China to attend my graduation, the only time they've ventured out of Beijing. They found Boston a bit overwhelming, I'm afraid. Tell me about you...interior designer?"

"Oh, Susan, I'm sooo over my head. But it's an incredible opportunity, if I can pull it off. I have to pull it off. The job could launch me on a rocket into the big leagues. Okay with you if I ask a few questions ...make that a lot of questions, about what it's like to live in China?" Jeli grimaced as she pulled a pad of paper in front of her, pen poised.

"Look, instead of my talking, how about we walk and talk? I think a show and tell might help you more. I'll take you to a furniture store I found when I first rented my apartment. The owner specializes in Chinese items—furnishings for every room, drapery fabrics, artwork, and smaller accessory items my family likes to display for good luck. It's only one T-stop. We can wander around and I'll explain the meaning behind the items I think you might like to keep in mind for your designs."

"Sounds fabulous. Do you have time?"

"Sure, it will be fun. Let's take a coffee with us."

Chapter 8

———

SUNLIGHT STREAMED IN THE large windows lining the front of the furniture shop. The brilliance of the sun infused life to the items on display. Susan pushed open the door, Jeli close on her heels. The shopkeeper, her silver hair pulled back into a long braid, hustled up to Susan, the pair exchanging a greeting that Jeli couldn't decipher but it was obvious they were happy to see each other.

Susan turned to Jeli, touching her arm. "Faye Yoon, I'd like you to meet my friend, Anjelica Bradley. She has a most important assignment. If you don't mind, I'd like to show her around."

"Be my guest, Susan. If you require my help, let me know."

"Come on, Jeli, let's start with the living room display. As you will note, the color red is very popular in the home. See the dragon woven into the fabric. The dragon is the most well-known symbol of China's cultural identity. It is the historical icon of the Chinese emperor, a symbol of power and masculinity. You will see it often in fabrics as well as statues.

"On the wall is a picture of cute monkeys. The Chinese New Year occurs after yours. This year, the year of the monkey begins on February twenty-fifth. Faye Yoon is very clever and has already hung the picture. The picture is considered appropriate Feng Shui, the practice of aligning one's physical environment with nature."

"Anything I can help you find, Ms. Bradley?" Faye said, joining Susan and Jeli. "Please, tell me about your assignment."

"I'm working with a developer, Josh Greely. He's renovating a building into condos. He has a prospective buyer coming from China. He says if the client approves it, it could lead to more sales from China...do you know him?"

Jeli caught a slight rise of the shopkeeper's brows.

"I've heard of Mr. Greely."

"I promised to have my ideas, a presentation ready for him, on Sunday. Susan suggested I get a feel, a look at what the client might like. The condo is to be completed and staged when the client arrives."

"I see," Faye said looking from Jeli to Susan. "I agree it could lead to other clients. Family is everything to the Chinese. It is more than likely others will follow in the footsteps of the family member. How will you present your ideas to Mr. Greely—paper, or on the computer?"

"Oh, definitely the computer. I have so little time to pull together my design, and I'm sure Mr. Greely will have ideas, changes, he would like. I'll incorporate his ideas immediately."

"Good. You obviously are clever—"

"I don't know how clever I am, but with the time constraint and—"

"Come back to my office before you leave. I'll show you the shop's website. With Susan's help, you can pick out furniture, accessory items. I'll put pictures of the items you might select on the site. You can then access them as you build your presentation, paste them in."

"Faye, that would be beyond wonderful. Thank you, thank you."

"I'm pleased to help you and besides, I help you, you help me. Maybe your Mr. Greely, or his client, will purchase some of the items from my shop."

"Faye, I've heard red is considered lucky. You feature red everywhere. Should I be aware of overdoing it?"

"No, no. The color red symbolizes luck and is believed to ward off evil. So, I doubt you could use it too much, but you're right to keep it in balance. Yellow and green are also considered to be lucky. Yellow and white are considered standard colors. Colors pop against a white wall, or yellow, or a creamy mix. Now, go look around, make a note if you want me to add something to the website."

"Thanks, I will. And I'll certainly steer Mr. Greely to your shop. I do have a question."

"What is that, Ms. Bradley?"

"Would you consider putting some of your pieces on loan...like if I suggested something to Mr. Greely as staging when his client arrives?"

"I would be happy to. I have a truck...we can drop off and pick up. At your convenience."

Jeli smiled, unable to help herself, giving Faye a quick hug, backing away just as quick, afraid she had offended the shopkeeper. She was relieved to see a broad smile on Faye Yoon's face.

"Come on, Jeli," Susan said. "Let's circle the shop once more, take a look at Faye's website, and then go to the café a few doors down. You can regroup. Ask me whatever you like over another cup of coffee."

Glancing around from one item to another, asking Susan questions, Jeli warmed to the charm, the calm of the shop. While patterns and some of the wood, the delicate carving, were foreign to her, there was a feeling of peace. The furnishings absorbed the sound, cloaking their voices to a whisper.

———

JELI DIDN'T SAY MUCH as Susan led her to the café. They asked for two coffees and settled at a little window table.

"Susan, I can't believe how helpful this has been...Faye practically built my presentation."

"Her help was very much the way Chinese do business."

"How's that?"

"I scratch your back...you scratch mine."

"I was afraid I had offended her when I gave her a hug...you know—the brash American."

Susan laughed. "Faye has been in the States many years. Your hug was interpreted as a compliment, an act showing you held her in high esteem. Would you like to show me your presentation tomorrow?"

"I wanted to ask you, but you've been so generous with your time...I don't want to impose."

"Nothing of the sort. Here's my cell number. Give me a call when you're ready."

"It's Sunday. I'm supposed to meet Greely early. But maybe I can reschedule him to one o'clock. How about we meet at Marshall's? I'm hanging out with him for the next few weeks, until I see how this job goes with Josh."

"Oh, I don't think so. Marshall may not approve."

"Not approve? Nonsense. He thinks you're terrific. He said you were a big asset to his company."

Susan looked away. "Well, if you think he wouldn't mind. But you must be sure."

"Done. I'm so excited, I'll probably be up most of the night. Expect my call mid morning, 10ish. That will give me time to incorporate any changes you suggest."

"Okay." To Jeli's surprise, Susan popped up, hustling to the cashier and paid for the coffees.

Snatching her tote and shoulder bag off the floor, Jeli caught up with her. "Susan, this should be my treat, especially after all your help."

"Nonsense. My pleasure, Jeli."

Again, overcome with the warmth of her new friend, Jeli wrapped her in a quick embrace. In return, Susan smiled, much like the broad smile Faye had on her face when they left the shop.

———

BURSTING INTO THE CONDO, Jeli found Marshall at his desk, hunched over his computer, three screens displaying lines and lines of code. Tossing her tote and laptop on the couch she threw her arms around her brother.

"Hey, careful there. You about knocked me off my chair."

"No. I'm showing that I hold you in high esteem," Jeli said, giggling.

"I take it you liked Susan."

"Like? What's not to like? She was awesome. Now you have to excuse me, my presentation awaits. I asked Susan to come over tomorrow for a critique. You don't mind do you? She seemed to think—"

"Not a problem. I'm meeting with my IT guy at the office. So you'll have the place to yourselves."

Chapter 9

———

THE SOFT GRAY OF DAWN serenely swept away the black night. Not so Jeli's heart. No serenity there. Her heart was thumping. She had just saved for the umpteenth time, the design layouts for Greely. Snatching a few minutes sleep here and there during the night, only to jump up the minute her head hit the pillow with yet another idea, another tweak. She was running on high-test coffee.

Pacing as she waited for Susan, she paused at the panoramic view of the city—the first rays of sunlight pinging off the glass windows of the surrounding buildings. She felt the excitement, the hustle bustle of the city dwellers, living and working in the caves of old replaced with glass and steel structures piercing the sky to the sun, the moon, the stars.

Jeli was on the verge of joining them.

The door buzzer snapped her out of her exhilarating future. With a sharp return buzz, she opened the door waiting for Susan to step out of the elevator.

As the door slid open, Jeli rushed to her. A quick hug, she grasped her hand leading Susan laughing into Marshall's condo.

"Do you always greet your friends…"

Susan paused, as she shed her cape to the back of the couch. "Wow, this is quite a place. Did you help Marshall decorate?" she asked, stepping to the floor-to-ceiling picture window.

"To a point. He likes sleek, clean lines, no clutter. It needs a woman's touch, a few accessories, don't you think?"

"Maybe, but I have a feeling with Marshall's brain continually filling with computer code to protect our clients from cyber attacks, that at the end of the day to come here must seem like a sanctuary, a place to reload."

"Enough of your boss, I need your thoughts on my designs for Greely's Chinese client. Here, sit, sit."

Susan sat in front of Jeli's laptop, her hand on the mouse ready to scroll. Smiling, she looked up at her new friend. "You are a quick study, Ms. Bradley. Inserting the picture of the monkeys will immediately tell the client that you did your homework, that you didn't slap something together. You honor him, by making an effort to understand what pleases him."

"Keep going, look at each room. I don't want to suggest something stupid, something offensive."

Susan bent forward, studying each layout as Jeli poured fresh coffee into two mugs, setting one beside Susan. Jeli stood around the corner of the table so she could see which design Susan was looking at as well as her facial expressions—a frown, a quizzical look, a...

"Your capture of feng-shui elements is subtle, beautiful...there to observe but not hitting in the face." Susan laughed. "Really, Jeli? A chessboard, set to play, on the countertop of the island? Masterful. Chinese love chess, and the game you chose is fashioned with Chinese-designed pieces. Quite different from what you find in the game-board sections of the Boston stores."

"Oh, I wasn't sure. But this one was featured on Faye Yoon's website so I figured it was appropriate," Jeli said.

"My friend, you have married the American open concept with Chinese colors, fabrics. I wish I could be a fly on the wall when Mr. Greely's client walks into this condo."

"Any suggestions? Changes?"

"Not a one."

"Susan, I need some air, and maybe a bagel to sop up some of the caffeine I've had in the last twelve hours. Want to take a quick walk? Then I have to pack up for my meeting with Josh."

"A walk it is, then I'm off to work. My brainstorm during the night is not nearly as creative as yours, but I do want to try a different string of instructions."

Jeli had a tiny clue as to what Susan just said. After all she had taken a few programming classes during the phase when she was emulating her brother. But the thought of strings of code vanished as she ran through her designs again. Even though Susan hadn't picked up on anything that might jar the culture of the Chinese client, she still worried. And, her designs were sure to look foreign to Josh. She doubted he had looked into what might offend his client. Mr. Greely had concentrated on the bones, as he called them, of the building which were equally important. And she gave him credit for it. He had not cut corners as far as she could see. The renovation was well done.

After coffee the girls hugged goodbye on a street corner, both promising to keep in touch.

Jeli turned back to Marshall's condo building. She was suddenly very tired. A shower, a ten-minute power nap, and then off to meet with Josh.

Chapter 10

———

ALTERCATIONS WITH HIS father had become a daily event. But last night was particularly vitriolic, downright hostile. The very thought of it sent Josh's blood to the boiling point, jump-starting his day. The elder Greely was furious with his son, who he trained in building construction at his knee. The boy never saw the need for a formal education, wanted to strike out on his own. Josh only saw that his father wanted to dominate him, stifle his ideas, stifle keeping up with the latest trends. His father called them fads. His father threatened to disown him, threatened to make it impossible to start his own business as a competitor in the city.

Stalking around his first real project, the condo reno, waiting for his designer, thoughts of seeing the vibrant redhead poured fuel on Josh's already heightened blood flow. He peered out the front window. *Where is she? She rescheduled to one o'clock. Needed a few more hours she said. It's now one o'clock straight up.*

He checked his watch, looked out the window again. Finally, there she was hustling up the front steps, a large tote banging against her thigh, the wind catching her hair, the sun sending sparks of gold into the icy air. Josh pressed the button releasing the door before Jeli pushed the button for entrance.

He was waiting for her in the doorway of the condo. As she rushed up to him, her emerald eyes smoking hot, he placed his hands on her shoulders, bringing her to him, planting a searing kiss on her ruby lips. She tasted good, smelled sweet. Releasing her, he pulled her into the construction site. "Look how much progress the workers made. Drywall up on three walls, and, as you suggested, the wall between the living room and kitchen knocked out ready for the island. What do you think? Nice?"

Flustered, her brows hitched at his greeting, she did as he said, turning in a circle to see how much had been accomplished. Not only was the drywall up, but it was taped and spackled, ready for paint. Large bundles of wood flooring were stacked in the center ready to be laid. "It's beautiful. Look at the sun filling the space."

"I thought you'd like it. Let's go next door. You can show me your ideas. I put on a pot of coffee." Josh bolted through the door, down the short hall to the raw unit he was going to occupy, make that *was occupying*.

Jeli followed quickly on his heels, her face still flushed from his passionate greeting.

Chapter 11

———

STEPPING THROUGH THE DOOR, the first thing Jeli noticed was a blowup mattress topped with a sleeping bag, a card table with two chairs, then the aroma of fresh-brewed coffee. Thrown off balance with his kiss, she took a deep breath, focused on setting her laptop on the card table, along with a pad of paper for notes, and a pen.

Where was that pen?

Digging around her tote, digging under her brush, wallet, she came up with the pen.

Pressing the start button on the computer, she leaned the tote against the leg of the chair and sat down. Josh set a mug of coffee to her left and pulled the other chair to her right so he could see the screen. Jeli didn't dare pick up the mug of coffee for fear her hand would shake. Opening the presentation, she took another deep breath, focused on the display releasing the tension in her body.

The picture of playful monkeys filled the screen.

"In China, 2016 is the Year of the Monkey. I thought this picture would be nice on the wall as your client entered, breaking the ice so to speak, aware that you had prepared the space just for him."

Josh didn't say anything, his eyes intent on the screen.

Jeli continued the presentation, scrolling through pictures of furniture, accessories, layout and lighting. A mockup of the rooms displayed with wall colors, drapery fabric, and small graphics representing furniture—tables, chairs, couch, beds. The file included the kitchen design with appliances and the placement and size of the kitchen island with stools on the living room side.

Absorbed in describing her ideas, the why of every element she had chosen, she relaxed. At the end she returned to the opening screen—the monkeys, 2016, Happy New Year.

Josh shoved his chair back, hands on his hips, he paced out to the hall, to the construction site. Again, Jeli followed on his heels, grabbing her computer on the way, stashing pad and pen in her tote.

"Look, if you don't like my ideas, we can discuss alternative—"

"Where did you get the furniture?"

"Online...well, from Faye Yoon's Furniture. A friend introduced me to her. I learned a lot about Chinese culture, what they like in their homes. You can visit her website. She was very helpful and said she would be glad to stage the condo for your client...free of charge."

"Nothing is free, Red. Ms. Yoon does a favor for you and expects a favor in return. It's the Chinese way." Josh paced around what was to be the living room, through the kitchen, around the island-to-be. He stopped at the front window looking down on the street, his back to Jeli. "I work with a Chinese furniture shop. The owner expects to stage the area but..."

"I'm sorry, I didn't know. Faye is aware I was presenting my ideas to you, so I'm sure she won't be offended—"

"Actually, we can use your new friendship with Yoon. It's all a matter of negotiation. We play one off against the other."

"Oh, I don't know. Both could be offended and we'd end up trying to find a third specializing in Chinese furniture. I can go to your friend—"

"No, no. I'll handle my contact."

Leaning against the wall, arms crossed over her chest, Jeli looked to the ceiling a puff of air escaping her lips. Maybe she was still on the job. "What do you think of the ideas?"

"Perfect. Everything was perfect. I need paint colors by ten o'clock tomorrow. Give me your cell number...I'll text you the store I do business with, the contact. Tell Customer Service that Joshua Greely Jr. sent you. They'll take care of you. Don't worry about paying. I'll take care of it. Just tell them to put the order on my account. Only deal with the contact I give you."

Josh remained at the window, cell phone in hand, tapping.

Hearing her phone ping, Jeli pulled it from her pocket as several texts lined up.

"When you've selected the paint, come back here with the chips—several of each color. The painters will be here. After the paint, the floors will be laid, then the molding. Tomorrow afternoon we'll go select the countertops. You have my text— company and contact. Oh, and give me the design of the island, the dimensions for my contractor. Once I have all the construction scheduled, you can negotiate with Faye Yoon. Not the final negotiation, but enough to give me a list, placement, and of course pictures of your choices. That way she will be sure to have the items in stock, ready to deliver, to stage."

Blinking, taking in Josh's rapid fire orders, Jeli stood prioritizing in her mind everything he had said.

He whirled suddenly to face her. Smiled. "Don't stand there, Red, it's time to prepare for tomorrow. Use the internet, the websites of the companies I gave you—match up the paint colors with your design, etcetera, etcetera." His words trailed behind him as he strode out of the construction site to his man cave next door.

Jeli heard the door bang shut.

Looking at the space where he had stood, hands on her hips, a scowl crossed her face. Mr. Josh Greely was the most complex, irritating, exciting man she had ever met. So, he was a junior Greely. She'd check that out along with the paint colors and countertops.

Pulling on her parka, stashing her laptop in her tote, she left the building. The sun was low in the skyline, losing the warmth she felt earlier. Her steps were slow, mechanical. The lack of sleep, and sapped of adrenalin, she finally made it to the T-stop.

The only thing on her mind was curling up on Marshall's futon with a mug of hot chocolate, the blanket, and a pillow—in that order. *No, change that—swap the hot chocolate for a glass of wine.*

Chapter 12

———

THE DREGS OF THE afternoon coffee languished in the bottom of the pot. His mind a jumble with Jeli's designs, Josh set another pot to brewing.

So much was riding on a quick sale. Josh didn't know what was going to happen first—selling the condo so he could pay off the loan with enough left to roll the balance into another property, or the flip side which meant defaulting on the loan and losing the property. One way or other he was going to make the first scenario happen. Failure was not in his DNA.

With the progress of his contractor, and Red's designs for the finish work and the staging, it was time to nail down the client from China. He had Quin Shi's cell number, the realtor representing the man. She never dropped her realtor mantle, even on a Sunday. Josh had to verify that the deal was still in play. Snatching his cell off the table, he didn't hesitate to place the call.

Shi answered on the first ring.

"Wéi, Quin Shi."

"Quin, Josh Greely. The client you suggested for my condo property, I have an approximate date for the showing. I'm confident I can meet it. You can move ahead—"

"Mr. Greely, I was about to call you about my client, Mr. Wu."

Quin Shi's voice rose to a high pitch, a pitch Josh was accustomed to when speaking with her. He was not accustomed to her heavy perfume, preferring to communicate with her over the phone. He sometimes wondered if her perfume was off-putting to her clients.

"What's the matter? He didn't buy something else did he?" Josh said.

A quick laugh, as Shi replied. "No, on the contrary, he is most anxious. You heard about the fall of the Shanghai stock market?"

"No, I've been up to my neck with contractors and designers."

"The big reason Mr. Wu is so anxious to see your property is to liquidate his money from the market and invest the funds in a piece of real estate in the States, particularly the Boston area. Of course, I steered him to you. And, you so kindly agreed to show him your property. How soon will it be ready?"

"Two weeks, three weeks to be safe—end of January. Will it be possible for him to travel that quickly? I wouldn't want him to miss out."

"Miss out? Mr. Greely, I thought you and I had an agreement. Surely you are giving my business priority?"

"Of course, I am, Quin."

"With the Chinese stock market tanking, and talk of the government devaluing the Yuan, I have many Chinese clients clamoring for property, no matter the price—high, low, somewhere in the middle. But they do want quality. Mr. Greely, you are clever, renovating property at a mid-level price. This will also save you money, no need to spend so much on materials for the high end while maintaining high standards. High-end market will come as you sell some properties, roll them each time to the next level up. You will be like your father—"

"Ms. Shi, I am not like my father. Remember your promise."

"Of course, I remember. I have said nothing to your father of our deal. Although, he would not be happy if he knew I had joined with you. But he is not taking advantage of my talents, my contacts, my negotiation expertise in bringing investment business from China at this time of market turmoil."

Josh rolled his head back, shutting his eyes, determined to keep his temper under wraps. Quin seemed to go on and on, not realizing she had made the sale. He was not going to another realtor. He had scouted the local agents for the one with the best network of investment companies, clients in China and settled on Quin Shi. She was particularly well known for her ability to work the Chinese real estate market in Beijing.

"Okay, but don't forget. Your discretion in keeping our relationship to yourself is crucial. Any breach and our deal will end. Let me know the date Mr. Wu will arrive."

"I will. It seems he has a grandson in Boston. The boy works for a computer firm and so Mr. Wu plans to stay with him while looking at properties. Family is everything to Mr. Wu. His grandson is the main reason I was able to garner his business. Mr. Wu, above all else, wanted to be near him."

"I'm sure he will be pleased with my condo, as you say it will be in his price range."

"Mr. Wu is a frugal man but I believe he has more wealth than he is letting on. Like you, he wants to start low, see how it works out. I feel he might be a good conduit to other family members...if he is pleased with your design."

"I'm sure he will find my property to his liking. Bye."

"Bái bái, Mr. Greely."

Chapter 13

———

A BLUSTERY WIND SWEPT through Boston's canyons of commerce. The biting twenty-one degrees stung faces, legs, anything that wasn't covered. Jeli zipped her parka to the top, purple scarf covering her mouth, but the frigid air still managed to gain access to her body. Climbing on the bus she huddled with the other passengers for warmth. Hanging onto the pole for balance, watching the street signs, she spotted the building supply company as the bus whizzed by. Thankfully it stopped at the end of the block.

Striding down the street, head bent against the biting frosty air, she managed to avoid any icy patches. Yanking the door, she stepped into the warmth of the store.

With the holidays left behind only a few days ago, Jeli was surprised at the number of people who had transitioned back to everyday life. Buyers crouched in the aisles to find items on the bottom shelves, others on tiptoe to reach what they wanted above their heads.

The paint department was particularly busy—nothing like a fresh coat of paint on the walls to kick off the new year. Jeli had a keen eye for color, picking out the paint chips she wanted in short order. Holding them in her fist, she made her way to the flooring section to pick out the tile for the kitchen and bathrooms and to check hardwood flooring samples. Nothing jumped out at her, so she decided the bundles of wood she saw ready to install in the condo that Josh had selected were complimentary with her designs. The assorted samples, representing hundreds to a few thousand dollars, didn't cover the bottom of her cart. Setting her tote in the child's seat, Jeli backed up against a display of carpet samples and called Josh.

Images of the rooms were rocketing through her mind—windows, walls, floors—transformed with her samples, when Josh answered his cell.

"Hey, Red. Trouble finding the store?"

"No trouble. All good. I'm ready with the SKU numbers for the paint and tile. They're listed on the email I just sent you. Note them on the layout I forwarded to you this morning. Will your contractor figure out the quantities—cans of paint, tile for kitchen and bathrooms?"

"Yes. Go to Customer Service. Tell them they'll be receiving a large order that I want delivered ASAP. Today."

"Wow. Today? How can they do—"

"Tell the manager that it's an urgent order for Joshua Greely. Put it on my account. Red, I'm emailing you the company that handles salvaged kitchen and bathroom cabinets pulled from renovation sites. They specialize in rescued countertops. If we find something we can use, we'll save boatloads of money. Then you redesign the kitchen to fit what we find. We'll meet up tomorrow at the shop."

"What time?"

"They open at seven. Once we see what they have, you can fit everything together. By the end of the week my crew should be ready for the install—cabinets, fixtures, etcetera, etcetera."

Jeli looked at her phone. He had hung up. "Josh Greely, you are the most ill-mannered, bossy person I've ever met. How do you expect—"

"Can I help you, miss." A clerk, covered in a black bib apron, stood in front of her.

"Customer Service?"

"Down this aisle, on your right."

"Thanks." Jeli pushed the cart at a fast clip. "Keep your eye on the prize, Jeli-bean, as Finn would say. Do this job, talk it up on your resume, and move on. Leave Mr. Josh Greely in the dust. There'll be other games in town," she muttered.

Jeli hit the little knob on the bell at the Customer Service window. A portly woman appeared on the other side looking over the top of her glasses. "Can I help, you?"

"Yes. Mr. Josh Greely asked me to let you know he'll be sending you an order, an urgent order, for paint and tile flooring. He needs it as soon as you can deliver it—this afternoon. The address is..."

Jeli retrieved her phone, her finger pushing the display to the text Josh sent with the condo's address the first day she met him. Years ago?

"Patriot Drive?"

Jeli looked up. "Yes, that's it. How did you—"

"I just received a text from him."

"I see. By any chance is there a furniture outlet nearby?"

"Next block. But if it's furniture for Mr. Greely, he deals with Alex Chen, Antique & Contemporary Asian Furniture. At least for his project on Patriot Drive. If it's for another site, he has a couple of other stores—"

"No, it's for the same project. Can you give me directions to Alex Chen's—"

"Let me write it down. Taking the bus?"

"Yes."

———

JELI STOPPED BRIEFLY IN the antique store, spoke briefly with Alex Chen, and left. She didn't linger because suddenly Mr. Chen appeared to be upset by something she said. Before braving the cold she sent a text to Marshall, asking if she could borrow his jeep. She had to go back to the farm for some more warmer clothes. He texted back, giving her where he kept a spare car key and asked if she was going to stay at the farm for a couple of days.

Her eyes bulged at the question. A few days? Hardly. She texted—*Quick round trip. Back by eight tonight.*

Sighing, she began muttering. "I can do this. I can do this. Jeli-bean, your days as a student are over, no more taking life for granted."

Now on Interstate 95 North to New Hampshire, Jeli told the car's phone device, to call Sadie, a trick Marshall showed her months ago. Waiting for Sadie to answer, Jeli switched lanes. Her exit was coming up.

"Hi, Jeli, how's the job going?" Sadie asked.

"Frightening, stimulating, infuriating—"

"Wow, all that in a few days?"

"And more...I think I need some advice from my big sis, but not now. Do you know if Travis found anything on Josh Greely?"

"He did. Not much though. Ask that Siri friend in Marsh's car to call Travis. Better if you hear it from him."

"Okay, thanks...I'll be calling you soon...for a woman's advice."

"I'm here, Jeli. Call when you're ready."

Checking the speedometer, Jeli eased up on the gas, relaxing against the leather seat as she pressed a button on the steering wheel. "Siri, call Travis."

"Hey, Jeli, how's the job going?"

"Travis, I'm not sure, but I'm going a little crazy dashing about trying to do what Mr. Greely asks, no, not asks, orders me to do. Sadie said you had some information on him."

"Not much, I'm afraid. He's the only son, four sisters, of a wealthy family. His father built a construction business from scratch. Nothing much on Josh—like father like son. Both are named Joshua Greely, Senior and Junior. Junior works for his father—a family business. The son doesn't have a different address, so I guess he lives with mommy and daddy. Oh, I think he may go by Josh. Found a couple of Google hits on the name in articles about his father."

"Not any more, Travis. He just moved into the condo adjacent to the one he hired me to layout the interior design work. He has a client from China coming to Boston the last week in January, or first week of February. I'm staging the condo for a showing."

"China? That could mean big bucks. I hear the real estate market in New York City and Boston is hot, foreigners investing, snapping up U.S. properties. Watch yourself. Gotta run."

"Watch—"

Travis was gone.

Glancing at the rearview mirror, she caught her image. "Watch myself? What does that mean? The store accepted Josh's order. He may be rude but they didn't say no to his business. Credit must be okay." Jeli chuckled. "A member of a mob? No way. Keep going, Jeli-bean. You don't have any money invested—only your time."

Chapter 14

———

WHIZZING INTO THE farmhouse kitchen, Jeli threw a kiss at her mom and Gran, and raced up the two flights of stairs to her room. Digging into the back of her closet, she pulled out her boots. Scrutinizing the fashion statement—soft black suede, high heels— her brows pinched together, lips hitching up on one side. Given the last few days, slipping and sliding after each snowfall, melting, freezing, she needed safety, warmth and comfort, in that order. The ones she picked up on the last trip weren't doing the job. Remembering the no-nonsense, flat-heeled boots lined with lamb's wool, she saw in the attic, she set fashion aside.

The attic was shadowy, only a hint of light penetrating the frosty window at the far end.

Where had she seen the boots?

Squinting, glancing to her left, a patch of light hovered over a box a few feet away. A warm feeling washed over her arm as she knelt beside the box. Pulling up the crisscrossed flaps, there they were—practical ladies boots. They were going to be perfect. Standing up, she saw something next to her foot. For a split second she felt a warm hug—or was it a chill? Stooping, she picked up a pair of red and black argyle socks.

"Rosemary...?"

Jeli's eyes roamed through the shadows. Not much was left in the attic—a few boxes. A dress form gave her a start. Giggling, she swept the scary feeling away "Come on, Jeli-bean, your imagination is playing tricks." Turning to leave, she paused, "Have a nice day, Rosemary," she said, closing the door.

Returning to her bedroom Jeli packed a white Fisherman's cable-knit sweater, lined slacks, a few pairs of heavy crew socks, and furry earmuffs. Finished, she pulled the boots on over the argyle socks—perfect fit.

Gran and her mom were still in the kitchen as she clomped down the stairs with the large suitcase.

"Are you sure you can't stay for dinner, Jeli? Pot roast, carrots...we'd love to hear how—"

"In a few days, Mom. I promise. I have to get back to Boston before the snow picks up."

"All right. Did you find what you were looking for?"

Jeli smiled. "Yup...and I said goodbye to Rosemary. She led me to the boots," Jeli said, raising her foot, waving a boot in the air.

Jane rolled her eyes as she picked up a container of the slow-cooked roast and vegetables, tucking it under her daughter's arm. "A little dinner for you and Marshall. Your father and Wolfe are cleaning off the Jeep. Drive carefully...call me when you get there so we know you arrived safely."

"Will do. Love you both." Giving her mom and Gran a peck on the cheek, Jeli headed out the back door. Wolfe grabbed the suitcase, loading it in the car as Pops sidled up to his daughter. "This developer you're working for, he has a client?"

"Sure does, Pops. A man from China eager to invest in a property."

"This Chinese man lives here now?" Wolfe asked.

"Not yet. But I've been told he's anxious to get his money out of their stock market. And, he's afraid the Yuan is going to be devalued. I learned a little about the market in China from my new friend, Susan Li. She's a programmer. Works for Marshall and a super nice person. Anyway, if the Chinese guy buys the condo, he'll put his money to work here in the States."

"And you're decorating the place?" Wolfe asked.

"You got it...decorating and at the same time trying not to do something disrespectful—our cultures are so different."

"If anyone can bridge the divide—Chinese to American—you can. I'd put my money on you any day," Pops said.

"Thanks, Pops. I'll keep you posted."

Jane watched out the back door at Jeli exchanging a few words with Pops and Wolfe, and Georgie as he came running to join the send off. Laughing, they exchanged hugs, kisses, and then she was gone, honking as she turned out of the driveway heading east to Interstate 95 and south to Boston.

Chapter 15

———

BUNDLED UP IN THE Fisherman's sweater, flannel-lined slacks, and argyle socks pushed into what she now referred to as Rosemary's boots, Jeli entered the salvaged building supply shop to meet with Josh. Their mission—pick out counters and cabinets for the kitchen and bathrooms.

She spotted Josh, his hand running over an island topped with granite.

Dropping his hand, he looked up as she approached. "What the hell were you thinking?"

"Excuse me. Hello to you, too. What's the matter?"

"Alex Chen called. Threatened to never work with me again."

Jeli's brows arched. "Why would he say that?"

"Oh, I don't know, maybe because you said you worked with me, maybe because you said you were doing business with Faye Yoon."

"First of all, it just came out that I was scouting for furniture for a Mr. Greely. And yes, that I had visited, as *dropped in, not doing business with*, Yoon's Furniture."

"I distinctly remember telling you not to visit my contacts. How did you know about Chen anyway?"

"Oh, well, the big reveal slipped out in my conversation with the paint customer service woman. I asked if there was a furniture dealer close by...she mentioned Chen...I guess."

"You, me, Yoon's furniture—it doesn't take a genius to connect the dots," Josh snapped. "Are you trying to sabotage my project?"

"Josh, don't be so paranoid. Mr. Chen must be very insecure if the mere mention of a competitor throws him into a tizzy. Now, are we going to pick out cabinets or not?"

The manager of the salvage store walked away leaving his customer to argue with the woman standing her ground. Noting that Josh had stopped talking and was staring at the young woman he had been quarreling with, the manager took the opportunity to call out, waving to Josh to inspect a group of white cabinets.

Jeli was fuming inside. How dare he snap at her, and in front of the manager. I'm going to have a chat with that man, give him a piece of my—

"Hey, Red, come look at these cabinets. They look identical to the ones in your design. Perfect in fact."

What was this? His idea of an apology? Okay, he gets a pass, but if he ever...

"I'm coming."

———

JELI AND JOSH SETTLED on the cabinets, along with the island and countertops, and scheduled delivery for tomorrow. Jeli had to nail down the furniture and accessories with Faye Yoon, the latest additions from her website, and check that everything was in stock—again. With that done she might even have time for a real lunch break.

"Josh, I'm going to Yoon's Furniture. It's critical the pieces for the staging are available to be delivered the minute your realtor gives you the exact date for the showing. Unless you have something else for me to do, I'll meet you tomorrow at the condo when the cabinets and the island arrive."

Pleased with her handling of Josh and the ruckus between the furniture dealers, Jeli broke into a grin morphing to a genuine pearly-teeth-flashing smile. Her head tilted one way, then the other, in a mock conversation with her employer. She no longer felt like it would be the end of the world if Josh fired her. As she saw it, he couldn't fire her. He was under the gun to finish the condo in time to show the client. There was no time to hire another designer, plus she had made many changes—new ideas she had, and directives he gave her. These changes were incorporated into the schemes on her laptop and he didn't have the most up-to-date file. And, he didn't know the newest pieces she had chosen for the staging. All he really had were the paint colors and tile samples.

Yup, she was looking out for herself, looking out for number one as Sadie would say.

Josh let out a long puff of air. "Keep your cell handy in case I need you. Stay away from Chen's furniture. No more sabotage."

"I hardly think stopping into his shop can be considered sabotage." Jeli smiled sweetly at the manager of the salvaged cabinets, and walked out sure-footed in her comfy boots.

Comfy feet or not, the frigid wind had not let up. She ducked into a café down the street for a mug of coffee and to make two quick phone calls, bracing for the next trip on the T-bus to Yoon's furniture.

She called Faye Yoon first to tell her she was coming to place the order for the staging—free staging. Then Jeli called Susan Li hoping to cajole her to meeting at Yoon's. Jeli didn't want to accidentally pick something that would offend Josh's client. The whole job was turning out to be a game, a game she planned to win. And to win she had to have the right players, and the right designs, or the game would suddenly end with the client leaving because she had been disrespectful.

Susan was more than happy to help and even suggested they have lunch after meeting with Faye.

With new vigor in her steps, Jeli's energy, her chi as Susan would say, was flowing in the right direction as she entered Faye Yoon's shop. Susan swept in a few minutes later, buffeted by the wind.

Jeli had compiled a final list of items she felt would set the stage, so to speak, for a successful showing of the condo to Josh's client. Susan suggested a few changes, and Faye said she would call tomorrow after checking, once again, on the delivery of all the pieces to her shop. She was sure there wouldn't be a problem. But, if there was a snafu, she thought she could replace it with one of her contacts in New York City. There was no mention of a spat with Alex Chen.

The meeting with Faye was short, and lunch with Susan was fun-filled with girl talk. The new friends giggled in the cozy, warm café. Inside or out, the café was a picture worthy of a magazine cover depicting a beautiful winter scene—lace curtains held back with green and red plaid ribbons, patrons bundled with earmuffs, wool scarves flying in the stiff wind.

———

THE FOLLOWING DAYS LEFT the positive chi under snow banks, snow banks that would melt washing everything down city drains to the sewer.

One of the painters dropped a bucket of paint from the top of the ladder in the bedroom, splashing blue paint over the new flooring. An industrial cleaner was called in for an emergency scrubbing. He said he was sorry, but was booked up. He thought, *maybe*, he could be there the next day, or day after, but couldn't promise.

Josh yelled at the painter, who turned on his heel leaving in a huff. The contractor called in another painter to finish the job but the guy couldn't make it today. Jeli figured, worst case, the bed along with a throw rug would hide the pale-blue paint splatter. She placed a call to Faye asking her to add the rug to the list, light blue to match the quilt she was providing. Ten by twelve feet should do it.

Jeli was about to hang up, when Faye told her the round rosewood table was not available. Her assistant had sold it earlier in the morning, and it had been delivered. Faye was hopeful she could find a replacement—if not from the New York shop she trusted, then San Francisco. Delivery would be close, but within the hour she'd find out if it was possible.

A thought came to Jeli—why would Faye go to such lengths to fill the order...free of charge. There was a chance the client would buy the condo furnished, but it was only a chance. No guarantee.

The thought evaporated when the cabinet man called. His truck had a flat tire. He was running late.

Finally, the cabinets were delivered, stemming the flow of bad chi. They were installed along with the island. The effect was stunning—white cabinets, charcoal quartz counters with specs of crystal, back splash a mosaic of hexagon tiles in black, white, and light gray. Walls were painted a soft pearl gray enhancing the pop of colors—Chinese red, greens, yellows, soft blue in the bedrooms. The chipped, red brick fireplace was refaced with white marble tiles.

The renovation was back on track.

Chapter 16

———

THE FARMHOUSE HAD LOST some of its sparkle since the youngest member returned to Boston. It was such a quick visit last week—picked up some clothes—in and out. This Sunday morning's breakfast, the familiar sound of forks on plates, was not the same as the family quietly planned the day's activities. Going to church was at the top of the list.

Pops heaved a sigh.

"What's the matter, dear? You seem preoccupied." Jane said as she passed the platter of scrambled eggs to Wolfe and Georgie. Gran looked up as she added a bit of salt to her eggs.

"Oh, I'm just concerned over what Jeli may be getting involved with," Pops said.

"Do you mean the developer—" Wolfe began to say.

"Or, is there someone new in her life we don't know about?" Georgie chimed in.

"It's not so much who she's working for, more about the job. Just before she left to go back to Boston the other day, I asked her about what she was doing, the job. Seems a fellow from China doesn't trust the Chinese stock market, wants to get his money out, and so he's looking to invest his funds in U.S. property. Specifically, the condo Jeli is decorating for her boss."

Gran folded the newspaper open to the business section, tapping her finger on an article. She slid the paper over to Jane. "Read this to us, Janie. It's an editorial. Exactly what Danny is talking about."

Jane set her coffee mug aside, straightened her glasses. "Okay, says here...Danny, are you listening?"

"Yep, go ahead."

"On both January fourth and seventh the Chinese stock market experienced a sharp sell-off of about 7% that quickly sent stocks tumbling globally. From January fourth to the fifteenth China's stock market fell 18% and the Dow Jones Industrial Average was down 8.2%.

"On January fourth, stock markets in China fell to the point of triggering its new trading curb rule, a market mechanism that halts trading when losses reach a threshold, which is intended to help stabilize stocks. During the first fifteen minutes of trading the stock market fell by 5% before regulators halted trading. It was reopened for another fifteen minutes and stocks fell until trading was again halted.

"On January seventh, Chinese authorities suspended the circuit breaker rule out of concern that the trading curb may have intensified investors' concerns."

Jane took a sip of coffee as she slid the newspaper back to Gran.

Gran leaned back in her chair. "Sounds to me like our little girl is in to something big, like in very big money."

Chapter 17

———

EVERYTHING APPEARED TO BE on track for the showing.

Josh's realtor, Quin Shi, called to say Mr. Wu had finalized his travel plans. He was arriving in three days and planned to stay in Cambridge with his grandson, Charles Wurthy. The man from China was looking forward to seeing the condo on January thirty-first, a Sunday. Seemed his grandson was overloaded at work and couldn't get away until then. Mr. Wurthy had insisted he accompany his grandfather, and Sunday was the day.

Bad chi returned.

The bay window replacement was delivered—five days late. Another arctic blast of air caught the edge of the large window. The installers lost control. The window fell, smashing into a million pieces on the sidewalk. The glass company scrambled to refill the order—two days?

Faye Yoon called. The display cabinet was back ordered. Fearful it would not arrive in time, she suggested a replacement. Susan Li answered Jeli's call for help and pronounced the replacement cabinet unsuitable. Jeli asked her to go to Alex Chen's shop, take a look, but under no circumstances was she to let on who it was for. Susan was to say she was purchasing the piece for her apartment.

Susan called late in the day. Chen had a perfect piece and would deliver it to her apartment—a lovely rosewood curio cabinet, with mirrored back. So, now the question was, how were they going to get it to the condo? Susan suggested Faye pick it up at her apartment and transport it to Patriot Street. But there was one problem. Chen's Furniture was stenciled in black on the back. If Faye Yoon saw the stencil she was sure to let Chen know, ha ha, where the cabinet ended up.

Jeli sighed. They would have to chance it.

January thirtieth arrived along with movers, painters touching up places they had missed, electricians installing the pendant lighting over the kitchen island, and the installation of the stove.

The stove was too wide and was immediately uninstalled.

A second stove was installed three hours later.

By midnight, Jeli, along with Susan, placed the last two accessories—an antique Chinese chess set on the kitchen island, and a small crystal ball on the coffee table providing positive chi— everything was in harmony with the two bedroom condo, fourth- floor brownstone, located on the outskirts of Boston.

Chapter 18

———

THEY WERE TEN MINUTES LATE.

There was sunshine, dry streets and sidewalks. No ice. So what was the delay?

Josh paced in circles—bay window, around the kitchen island and back. Quin Shi said she was bringing Mr. Wu to see the condo no later than eleven-thirty. Jeli stepped quickly between the front hall closet to the bedroom, living room, kitchen, back to the closet, double checking every detail.

"They're here. Quin just got out of her van," Josh said, peering out the window. "Stop fussing, Red." Josh ran down the stairs, bypassing the elevator, to greet his realtor with her client in tow. Opening the front door ready to say hello, shock crossed his face. A stocky bull of a man was hauling up a wheelchair, bump, bump, bumping against each step, a bird cage swinging from a hook on the back of the chair.

"Good morning, Mr. Greely. Sorry, we're running a bit late." Quin Shi called out from the sidewalk. A man stood next to her waiting for the wheelchair to crest the top step.

Josh couldn't see her. She was blocked by the sumo wrestler turning the wheelchair to face the front door. Jeli, bug eyed, peered around Josh. No one had mentioned that Mr. Wu was a cripple.

Josh was frozen in place, leaving Jeli to seize the moment. She squeezed around him to face the man in the wheelchair. *He had to be Mr. Wu,* she thought extending her hand.

"Mr. Wu, it's so nice to meet you," Jeli said, with a warm smile, gently shaking his hand, remembering Susan's words—Chinese like to shake hands, a sign of respect, but gently, not aggressively which is so typical of Americans greeting one another.

The grumpy face of the man in the wheelchair changed. A smile immediately crossed his face, reflecting Jeli's greeting. His face was round, eyes peeking out under heavy lids, returned the warmth of the young woman holding his hand. Silver gray hair fringed from under his cap.

Quin Shi squirmed around the wrestler leaving the other man on the sidewalk. "Mr. Wu, it is my pleasure to introduce you to the developer who has renovated a condominium just for you. And this woman...Mr. Greely, please introduce—"

"Yes, excuse me, Mr. Wu. This is Ms. Bradley, the interior designer for the project."

"Ah, Ms. Bradley, and the man down on the sidewalk is my grandson Charlie, Charles Wurthy," Wu said craning his neck to see the man standing on the sidewalk with a scowl on his face.

"Mr. Greely, if you'll show us the way, Mr. Wu's companion, Mr. Qiáng, will take him inside...out of the cold," Quin said, her body visibly shivering under her long coat.

Respect, respect, respect. Susan's words rang in Jeli's ears as she extended her hand to the burly man behind the wheelchair. "Mr. Qiáng, nice to meet you." Looking away, she addressed the man below. "And you too, Mr. Wurthy." The grandson, coal black hair, didn't look anything like his grandfather, except for the high cheekbones. Even from the top of the steps Jeli could see his large dark, very dark brown eyes, full lips under a hint of a mustache. A line of facial hair outlined his chin.

Josh turned, walked down the hall, staring at the open elevator door. Shock remained gripping his face, breath trapped. Jeli leaned against the doorframe.

"Quin Shi never mentioned her client was a cripple...the front steps are sure to be an obstacle to the sale. The grandson didn't look happy either," Josh muttered through his teeth.

"Did you catch that ring on Mr. Wu's middle finger?" Jeli said.

"Yes, when we shook hands—looked like he had it for a long time, worth thousands on today's market."

"Hard to miss, especially the diamond. Over a carat?"

"Maybe, but the gold is worth much more. I'll take it as a positive sign."

"Positive? In What way?" Jeli said.

"As a sign he can afford to buy the property...that he's loaded."

Chapter 19

Chinese Year of the Monkey

THE WHEELCHAIR ROLLED ACROSS the threshold into the condo. Wu instantly waved his hand signaling Qiáng to stop pushing. Wu leaned forward, his eyes trained up on the picture of the colorful monkeys in a bright red-lacquer frame.

Charlie glanced at Jeli. Feeling his eyes, she turned to him exchanging smiles. The year of the monkey had performed as she had hoped—welcoming Mr. Wu to his new home.

Grinning, a joyful rapid-fire exchange between Wu and Qiáng followed, as the companion removed the covering over the birdcage. A vivid blue and green parrot, orange breast, black hooked beak, cried out, "Hello, Charlie. Hello, Charlie." The birds claws clung to his perch swinging with each step Qiáng made manipulating the chair.

Crying out in English. Can he speak Chinese too? Jeli wondered.

"Mr. Wu, your parrot is beautiful. What's its name?"

"Thank you, Ms. Bradley. His name is Chang-ying—flourishing, lustrous. Fits, don't you think?"

Jeli smiled nodding her head. "He's very lustrous."

With a wave of Wu's hand, Qiáng continued into the living room. Wu pointed to the coffee table, to the dragon statue, the crystal ball. Wu called to Charlie, the pair exchanging comments in Chinese.

Jeli looked at Josh, raised her brows. So, the grandson converses with the grandfather in his native tongue.

Wu raised his hand, fluttering his fingers to Qiáng…go, go, go.

Jeli didn't know the foreign words, but she did recognize the almost gleeful body language of Mr. Wu, his grandson, and Qiáng. The monkeys had changed their moods—scowls to smiles.

Qiáng leaned around Wu's shoulder pointing to the island, whispering something into Wu's ear. The companion was pointing to the chessboard, the pieces positioned to begin play. Raising his eyes to the counter, Wu laughed.

"Ms. Bradley, come closer. You know I play chess?" Wu asked, as Qiáng placed the parrot's cage beside the chessboard.

"Play chess. Play chess." The colorful parrot followed the words with a blast of gibberish. *Chinese?*

Jeli moved to Wu's side, touched his arm. "I hoped you might. Wait, I'll put the board on the coffee table. Tell me if it's to your liking. I was told Chinese chess pieces are somewhat similar—"

"No. Leave it. Watch me." Another hand signal, and Qiáng moved the chair close to the counter. Wu pushed a button and the chair rose. It rose to the height as if Wu was sitting on the high stools Jeli had positioned at the counter for a casual meal, or, in this instance, a game of chess. "See, Ms. Bradley? Charlie and I can play chess here while Qiáng prepares dinner. Oh, Ms. Bradley, I am honored by your designs. Charlie, see the pickle jar? Like your aunt's. Do you remember what she told you?"

"Yes, Grandfather. 'When one man says the vinegar is sour, but the other says it is bitter, Confucius says the vinegar is both sour and bitter, the way nature intends pickles to taste, thus achieving social harmony between the two sides.'"

The old man nodded his head, waved his hand to Qiáng to continue the tour. The companion circled the chair in front of the bay window, the sill low enough so Wu could see the street below. Continuing around to the living room, to the coffee table between the fireplace and the couch, Wu signaled Qiáng to stop.

"Charlie, Ms. Bradley is very clever. A golden fish swimming in its bowl, centered on the table. Your aunt—"

"You're right, Grandfather. My aunt said, 'Fish attract prosperity to your home by flicking away bad luck with their tails.' And before you ask about the crystal ball on the coffee table, like the one my aunt took special care that it was spotless, she said 'it purifies and raises the level of positive chi in your environment.' I was quoting her. Did I get it right?"

"Yes, Charlie. You remember your aunt's words correctly. She was diligent in teaching you our ways. Qiáng, let's look at the other rooms. I believe we have an appointment to see another condo and we don't want to keep Quin Shi waiting."

Jeli and Josh turned to Quin Shi. Another appointment?

Quin shrugged her shoulders in reply.

Josh squinted at her, a dark look in his eyes. A shrugging of shoulders was not reciprocated. He was not happy. He wondered, had the two furniture dealers brought their spat to Quin? Was she thinking maybe he was talking to another realtor?

Charlie caught the looks flashing between the three—Shi, Greely, Bradley. Not commenting, he followed Qiáng to the two bedrooms, a full bathroom and a half bath. They returned to the living room pausing at a drawing Jeli had created. The drawing was from an architect's bird's eye view—a tree-lined street, curly wrought iron fencing—sidewalk on one side, a strip of grass bordered by winter-hardy plants with colorful leaves—bayberry, evergreens. It was signed in the lower right-hand corner, J. Bradley.

"Ms. Bradley, is this a print of your vision for this neighborhood?" Wu asked.

"Yes, it is. I don't have a copy with me. Do you have an email address?"

"Yes. Qiáng, write my email address down for Ms. Bradley, and then we must go."

The companion did as instructed, then picked up the birdcage, replacing the cover.

"Bye, Charlie. Bye, Charlie," the bird cried out as the cover slid over his cage.

Hanging back, Charlie pulled Jeli aside as Qiáng wheeled his grandfather into the hall.

"Ms. Bradley, thank you for all the work, your research into what would please my grandfather. He has two other appointments, but I doubt either will come close to what you presented."

"In case I don't see you again, Charlie, can you call me, let me know whatever your grandfather decides? If he decides against this condo, I'd like to know why so I don't miss the mark in the future. Here's my card."

"Is this your personal number? Mr. Greely—"

"I'm a freelance designer—interior design and architecture. Mr. Greely hired me as the interior designer for this particular job. This is my personal cell number."

"I will definitely call...one way or the other." Charles Wurthy extended his hand to her and then was gone.

Feeling a lurch in her stomach, at the warm touch of his hand around hers, Jeli turned to the living room's bay window. She watched Qiáng help his employer into the van, stashing the wheelchair in the back. Climbing into the backseat, Charlie looked up at the window, waved to her, and shut the van door.

"How fickle can I be," she muttered, returning Charlie's wave. "Face it, Jeli. You're drawn to handsome men."

Joshua marched into the condo, slamming the door. "Can you beat that? Quin is showing *my* client other condos."

Well, maybe not every man, Jeli thought watching the van turn the corner.

Chapter 20

MARSHALL'S CONDO WAS QUIET as a tree hollow, more than quiet, lonely quiet. Marshall had flown out Sunday morning on a business trip to Israel. Jeli decided to stay in Boston, hoping Josh would call with news that Mr. Wu had chosen his property. But two days had passed with no word. Faye Yoon's truck was scheduled to pick up the furniture and accessories, leaving the condo barren.

Jeli stared at her phone lying on the kitchen counter. Surely Mr. Wu had made a decision. She did receive a thank-you email for the street drawing she dropped off at Quin Shi's office to give to Mr. Wu, but that was it. Thank you—nothing more.

With all her efforts not to do something disrespectful, maybe she had without knowing. Charlie hadn't called either. "I guess I misread the spark I felt between us," she muttered, salting the fishbowl with fish food. "Good thing I brought you home with me, little fishy. No one else cares."

Looking out the window at the snow banks below, the icy street shimmering in the late afternoon sun left her wondering what she should do to break the stalemate. The excitement of the past four weeks had popped like a big old fat balloon pricked by an icicle. She was back at square one. So much for staying in Boston on the chance Wu decided on the property. If he did, it could mean another assignment. Or would it? Josh hadn't really talked to her about anything beyond this. Inferred there might be, but nothing definite. Or, had she stayed in Boston to see Charlie again. Sighing she turned away from the window. "Maybe I should call Susan. She'd be winding up her day soon. We could meet for—"

The saints were marching. Jeli darted to her phone.

It was Charles Wurthy.

"Mr. Wurthy. I was just thinking about your grandfather."

"Ms. Bradley, I'm sorry to call so late. Any chance you could meet me for dinner this evening?"

"I'd like that. What time and where?"

"How about seven o'clock? I thought somewhere around Quincy Market...someplace warm. Where do you live?"

"I've been staying with my brother, here in Boston, while I was working on the Greely property. I can take the T—"

"I have a better idea. Give me your address and I'll pick you up with an Uber driver."

"All right. I'll meet you out front. Give me a call when you're on the way."

"Will do. See you tonight."

———

THE UNION OYSTER HOUSE was bustling with office workers out and about, freed from their jobs, seeking a warm pub. Couples huddled in booths, some reaching across the table sharing words of love, others leaning back in easy conversation, or heated, over the day's events. The couple on the second floor, sat across the table from each other, a flickering candle flame mirrored in their eyes, taking in a developing friendship...maybe more.

They were on an island unto themselves.

Other patrons, however, took note of the pretty young woman, soft-gray silk scarf double looped over a bulky white sweater, her red hair crackling with fire and hints of gold. The handsome man, his charcoal gray turtleneck sweater over muscles formed in a gym or a taxing sport, fixed his dark brown eyes on her eyes of emerald green. He had a hint of a mustache over his warm smile.

A waitress poured white wine in sparkling goblets, excused herself, saying their order of clam chowder and slices of hot cornbread would be out soon.

"Charlie, stop teasing. I'm on pins and needles. Has your grandfather decided on a property?"

"Yes. He's making a quick trip to Beijing to secure his finances for the purchase."

"And..."

"And...he has chosen Greely's property."

Jeli's brows shot up, eyes crinkling over a broad smile. "Yeah! That's wonderful. I was afraid I had offended him with—"

"Offended? It was you who nailed the deal. He hasn't stopped talking about Ms. Bradley this, and Ms. Bradley that."

Charlie leaned forward touching his glass to hers. "Cheers," he said smiling as both took a tiny sip of their icy white wine.

Setting his glass on the table, his hand grasped hers, feeling her excitement. "You are an ambassador, a very beautiful ambassador. If I may be so bold to say, you're bridging the great divide between two continents, but not in distance, but of a human being wishing to take a monumental step of moving from one culture to another. I have wished for my grandfather to move to the States, to Boston, but I never dreamed he would. You did it, Ms. Bradley."

"Does Josh know?"

"By now, I think so. Quin Shi was going to call him." Charlie's eyes flicked over her face. "You call me Charlie. Can I call you something besides Ms. Bradley?"

"My name is Anjelica Jane Bradley, but please call me Jeli. When I was born, my baby brother, all of five years old, couldn't pronounce Anjelica, only Jeli."

"I think I like Anjelica—it suits you.

Jeli smiled, sipped her wine.

"Charlie...what do you do...here in Boston?"

He leaned back, fingered the stem of the goblet. "With my dual heritage—Chinese mother and American father—I'm privileged to speak two languages fluently, Chinese and English. My grandfather and father agreed I should be educated in the States. So from the age of five, I attended school in Boston. My father is head of a financial management firm...not far from here. Actually, it's his business. Summers and vacations, no matter if just a few days, were spent in Beijing. With my heritage, and my degree in computer science at MIT, I was courted by various companies, especially the past two years. Of course, the alleged computer hacking by the Chinese helped."

"Alleged? I've heard there's significant proof—"

"Yes, I'm afraid you've heard correctly. While it's not the main reason my grandfather wanted to relocate to Boston, it is one in the back of his mind."

"What's the main reason, if you don't mind my asking?"

"Money. He came into a large amount of money. A settlement of sorts. Before the money, he and my grandmother wanted a better life for their daughter and moved to Beijing from a poor farm in northern China. As he tells it, they struggled, financially struggled until the windfall."

Charlie paused, his mind appeared to wander and then he picked up the thread he dropped.

"The last two years have been chaotic in the Chinese market, to say the least. The latest sharp decline in the Shanghai financial market was the last straw. My grandfather is afraid he'll lose all of his money and wants to get it out of China as soon as possible."

"How awful for your family...but I'm secretly pleased to be part of his decision. I only hope he is happy with his choice. It can't be easy."

"What about you, Anjelica? You seem to be a spirited, adventuresome young woman."

Jeli felt the heat rising up her face. Something she couldn't control, an Irish trait from her mother. "I was raised on a farm, Lakeville, New Hampshire. Have you ever been to New Hampshire?"

"Only in passing—Route 95 into Maine. One of my fraternity brothers was from Maine. His parents had a cottage...a cottage that was as big as a hotel."

"I have three siblings, starting with the two oldest—twins, Sadie and Marshall. Then my baby brother, now forty, and then me...the real baby of the family. Oh, there are two other members of the family, though not blood related—Wolfe and his son

Georgie. We grew up with Georgie. He was a few months old when the twins were born."

"Sounds like a big family. Happy?"

"Oh my, yes. A rollicking, crazy-fun group, including my mom and pops, and pop's mother. We call her Gran." Jeli's eyes dropped to the goblet twinkling in her hand. "Charlie, when do you think your grandfather will take possession of the condo? Does he want any of the furnishings...sorry, I don't mean to talk shop. It's just I was the one who arranged for the staging from the—"

"He wants it all, down to the chess set, crystal ball—all the accessories. Very good chi he said."

"Even the goldfish?"

"Especially the goldfish," Charlie said, amusement in his voice.

"Hmm, yes. Positive energy. Faye Yoon, the furniture dealer, is going to be ecstatic. My friend Susan Li, she works for my brother's company, introduced me to Faye. They were both unbelievably helpful. Do you think it's okay if I talk to Faye Yoon, or...no. I'll call Josh first. I'm getting ahead of myself."

"There's something else you should know, Anjelica."

Jeli looked up. Charlie's eyes were soft, a bit amused.

"Mr. Greely may end up selling every unit in the building to my grandfather and his friends, extended family," Charlie smiled at the astonished look on her face.

"Furnished?" Jeli's brows went up, eyes popping big.

Chuckling, he replied. "That I don't know. But, if you're present at the realtor's showing, I wouldn't be surprised if they bought some pieces."

———

CHARLIE ASKED THE UBER driver to wait while he escorted the lady to the door.

Charlie held Jeli's hand as they walked to the security entrance of the building. Leaning against the plate glass, she turned to him. "Charlie, thank you for dinner, for introducing me to your amazing grandfather and...sharing some of your childhood. I do have one request...sorry, shoptalk again."

"Shoot."

"Will you let me know when your grandfather moves in? I'd like to welcome him."

"Consider it done, but it may be a few weeks. He's complaining about the stock market. Seems it's tanking on a daily basis. Anjelica, I'd like to see you again, before that. Have you been to the Boston Pops?"

"Once...the Fourth of July, their annual performance at the Hatch Shell."

"There's a concert next week at Symphony Hall. Would you like to go...dinner first?"

"Oh, yes, I would. I'll probably still be hanging out with Marshall, but if not, I'll take the T, meet you wherever you say."

"Good... Anjelica, I enjoyed tonight." Charlie kissed her cheek, squeezed her hand. He waited until she was safely inside and then strode to the Uber car, engine running, exhaust releasing plumes of frigid air.

Chapter 21

———

JOSHUA GREELY SENIOR SLAPPED the stack of invoices, statements of money owed, down on his desk. It was a large desk befitting a successful developer—dark mahogany polished to a glossy sheen. Hanging his suit coat in the closet, part of the private bathroom inside his office, he removed the gold cufflinks, rolled up his shirt sleeves. He then yanked the knot of his tie loose as he stared at his son.

Joshua Greely Junior had been summoned. With a smirk on his face, he stood before his father. His blue flannel shirt, tail out of his jeans, over a white turtleneck, he rocked in his western-style leather boots. Josh always wore western boots, feeling they added to his stature, in inches as well as demeanor.

Greely Senior's hair had long since changed from dark blonde to silver. Adding to the silver strands was today's confrontation with his son over his use of his father's name, his suppliers, his contractor accounts, racking up over $300,000 of debt. His face filled with fury, cheeks deep red, he glared at Josh. "How dare you pose as me...I called the bank, threatened to close my account if they didn't verify my signature in the future. Just how do you propose unraveling the debt you owe me? Tell me that! How?"

"I'll pay off every penny before it comes due...in person. As to how, I'll simply explain that you told me I was a full partner in Joshua Greely and Son, Real Estate Developers."

"That's a lie and you know it. You are never again to use my name to secure a loan, or a line of credit. Yes, I had hoped you would be part of the firm one day, but so far you've insisted on taking short cuts, always going behind my back. You also knew, I explicitly told you, that from here on out, you were on your own."

"And that's exactly what I did. The loan from the bank was for a property, a reno on the outskirts of Boston—"

"Yes, you told me about the property, and I distinctly *told* you it would be a money pit, a loser, a—"

"Excuse me, *father*, for breaking into your little tirade. I just sold the property for a nice profit, a profit that I will roll over into the renovation and sale of the other nine units in the building. In fact, I will be receiving deposits soon to fund the renovation of the units. So, I'm in the market for another property. Do you have anything to recommend?" Josh shot back.

"I'll tell you what I recommend. I recommend that you say goodbye to your mother, then get out of the house, and don't let the door hit you in the ass on your way out."

Josh turned on his heel, stalked out of his father's home office, out the front door, and drove down the circular driveway of the Greely estate. He decided not to say anything to his mother. She always sided with good old dad so there was nothing to add in rebuttal to his father's ultimatum. Besides it was getting late and he hadn't been able to reach Red to update her on Quin Shi's call—Wu was buying the condo.

Pulling into a strip mall, Josh tried to reach Red for the third time. He again left a message to return his call as soon as possible. This time he added to the message. "Wu bought the property. Maybe more. Meet me tomorrow night for dinner to celebrate, seven thirty, the Chart House."

———

JELI RODE THE ELEVATOR to Marshall's condo. Inside she leaned against the door thoughts of Charlie floating through her mind. It had been a lovely evening—fine wine, cod stuffed with lobster cooked to perfection, and a handsome man sitting across the table. The image of Charlie's face in the candlelight slid into her brain. He was intriguing to say the least. She'd guessed he came from a cultural mix somewhere along the way. His grandfather, of course Chinese, but tonight she learned his mother was Mr. Wu's daughter, his father an American living in Boston. Then there was the aunt. Jeli wasn't sure which side of the grandparents she fit in. He talked a lot about the aunt when he and his grandfather toured the condo, but tonight he mentioned his mother only once.

Sighing, she pushed away from the door noticing her cell blinking on the kitchen island. In her rush to get ready for her dinner date, she had forgotten to pick it up.

Not wanting to disturb the warmth of the evening, she shed her boots by the door, hung her coat on the coat tree's spike. Ambling to the open kitchen, she lit the candle on the island, and poured a small glass of wine to top off the night in style. Perching on the stool, she picked up the cell. There was a message from Marshall that he would be another week in Tel Aviv, and three messages from Josh.

Smiling, guessing why Josh was calling, she listened to the first of the three, then the second asking her to call. Listening to the last message he left confirmed what Charlie told her—his grandfather had chosen Josh's condo. Taking a sip of wine, smiling at the excitement in Josh's voice, her lips slowly turned to a frown. The difference between Josh's invitation to dinner and Charlie's was stark. Josh didn't really ask her to have dinner with him, he ordered her. And, there was no offer to pick her up. She had to get herself to the restaurant. *Oh well,* she thought, *different men, different ways of asking a woman out. Besides, Josh was very excited as he should be. She'd give him a pass this time.*

Chapter 22

———

THE CHART HOUSE WAS the oldest structure on Boston's Long Warf dating from the early 1830s. Built of red brick, the interior was reminiscent of historic times in Boston with rough hewn beams, and dramatic panoramic views of the Atlantic Ocean lapping the pier. Seamen secured their boats knowing a delightful meal was at hand before continuing their journey on the high seas. The restaurant was always a delight, a place Jeli had been to once before with Sadie and Marshall.

Discarding the casual look of last night, Jeli chose a bit more sophisticated—heels, wool slacks, and a soft, delicate, deep purple cowl neck sweater, the only somewhat dressy costume she threw in her suitcase at the last minute. Gold hoop earrings, a gold chain and locket picked up the hint of gold in her red hair in the candlelight.

The Uber driver pulled up to the front entrance, helped her passenger out of the car onto the brick sidewalk swept clear of snow and ice. Jeli paid the woman, and walked the few feet to the door stepping inside.

Glancing around, she didn't see Josh. Turning to the hostess, Jeli asked if Josh Greely had signed in for his reservation.

"Yes, ma'am. He's—"

"Thank you, he's coming down the stairs," Jeli said, smiling at the cocky blond man approaching.

Josh strode to her side pulling her into a quick embrace, his eyes sliding over her tip to toe.

"Ms. Bradley. Very pretty! My, my. Follow me. I have a table upstairs, tucked in the corner. Nice and private."

An ice bucket stood on a pedestal beside the table, a bottle of champagne chilling. His waitress, hustling to assist, took the champagne bottle from his hand. "Let me do the honors for you, Mr. Greely. Would you like to order now or—"

"Now please. We're starved. We'll both have whatever your special is—the lobster stuffed scrod, I believe you said. I'm sure it's wonderful." He glanced from the waitress to Jeli. "Nothing like a little lobster, eh Red?"

Blinking at the rush from the front door to the table, Jeli nodded. "Nothing like lobster, Mr. Greely," she said, her voice sticky sweet.

Over stuffed scrod, Joshua continued to tell Jeli his plans in animated detail. Finally sated, he pushed his empty plate to the side, hers on top of his. Reaching across the table, palms up fingers beckoning her to put her hand in his. She obliged as he gently ran his thumb over her fingers.

"I'm going to put diamonds on your beautiful hands, Ms. Bradley. I have to strike now. The next five years are key. After that, I don't know... but right now the Chinese are scrambling to get their money out of China. The market goes down every day. The Yuan is being devalued. And, I will be ready and waiting to sell property to them. I will be waiting to receive their Yuans exchanged for dollars."

Josh added the last of the champagne to their goblets. "First, I'll roll over Mr. Wu's money to renovate the other units in my building, with your help of course." Josh raised his glass to hers. "Like I said, five years and the street will be coming up roses. I'll have bought and sold everything. Then it will be time for the big leagues."

"Sounds like you'll already be in the big leagues. I mean...the whole street?"

"Quin Shi has lined up others in Mr. Wu's family and his network of friends. She says they want to live close, more of the condos like his. You saw the big fellow, I can't pronounce his name—you saw him take pictures. Well, when Wu returned to Beijing, he passed them around. And, there are other countries you know, their citizens eager to buy property in the States— Greeks, Brazilians, people living in Venezuela."

"All in Boston?"

Josh laughed. "No, no. We'll have to travel throughout the U.S., find cities where their fellow citizens have congregated, then we buy block after block so the Greeks can be with Greeks, Brazilians with Brazilians, or if they want to live somewhere new, we can do that."

"Sounds terribly ambitious, Josh. Lots of money. By the way, when do I get paid for the first condo?"

"Thought you'd never ask, Ms. Bradley." Josh reached in his pocket, removed a white business-size envelope, slid it across the table to her. "The first check of many."

"Josh, I accepted the money you offered for this job. You said, if it worked out, that there would be a bonus. Maybe even a raise?"

"Ah, Red, yes, a bonus, a raise, but only if you agree to the balance of condos in this building, ten total. One down, nine to go. After I turn over the first four, I should be able to buy up several of the buildings on the street. I have to keep it going...you understand don't you?"

"Yes, but, I may take other jobs. I think I can handle more jobs."

"What? Work for someone else at the same time? Oooh, I don't think so. Tell you what, help with three more, that would be the top two floors. Then we can discuss the rest. I think we might do something spectacular in the basement. The half-windows can look out onto a bed of flowers. What do you think?"

"I don't know. I haven't seen the basement."

Jeli found herself drawn into his vision for the street. By that time she would have a fabulous resume to present to clients, branch out on her own.

"So, Ms. Bradley, are you up to the challenge? A modest raise to complete the top two floors? Then double your pay as we move forward."

"Yes, Mr. Greely. Count me in." Catching his enthusiasm for the project, the next two years played out in her mind.

"Good, now let's be on our way. Did you drive tonight?"

"No, I took an Uber."

"Then I shall escort you home. You'll share my Uber."

Giving a credit card to the waitress, Josh asked her to call for an Uber taxi out front. The check paid, Jeli slipped on her tan car coat and gingerly navigated the stairs, the hall, and out the front door.

The crisp air was refreshing. The male driver held the door for her, Josh slid in behind her. She leaned forward, giving the driver her address.

Josh had swept her off her feet. The brash first few minutes, meeting him at the hostess station, were forgotten.

The driver pulled up to the curb, hopped out to help his passenger as she stepped onto the icy street. Josh popped out of the other door, nodded to the driver that he would be right back after escorting the lady to the door. Grasping Jeli's hand, they strolled to the entrance. He turned her to him, held her tight, planting a deep, passionate kiss on her ruby red lips. Leaving her speechless, Josh smiled as he turned away, calling over his shoulder. "Get some rest, Red. You're going to be very busy—the other units in the building, then the whole street. We're going to be rich."

Chapter 23

———

THE SECOND WEEK OF February ushered in a welcome reprieve from the sub-twenty-degree temperature Bostonians had been suffering. Jeli's purple scarf hung loosely around her neck. It seemed she had drawn the scarf over her lips forever, warming the air she breathed.

Without the urgency of a deadline, Jeli was restless. She needed, wanted to work, but wasn't sure if she should begin marketing herself as an interior designer. Josh made it clear he wanted exclusivity for one, two, maybe more years. Then there was Josh the man—she fed off of his excitement, felt at loose ends without the rush.

But it was Charlie she wanted to know about—his family and spending so much of his young life in China. She could learn from him, if, as Josh indicated, they were going to be doing business with people in Wu's network. Lots of business. "Who are you kidding? You just want to see Charlie. It's been several days and he hasn't called," she muttered, crossing the street to the café.

Frustrated, confused, she was in limbo waiting for Wu to return to Boston and close the sale, and baffled by her mixed feelings over the two new men in her life.

Needing to get a grip, gain some perspective, preferably from a female, she was eager to meet Susan Li for lunch.

Pushing the café door open, she spotted Susan sitting in a booth toward the back. Susan gave a little wave.

"Hey, girlfriend, that scarf is amazing with your green eyes. I ordered for us—two tuna on rye. With mugs of coffee, of course," Susan said grinning.

"Perfect. I'm going to leave my coat on for a bit. I can't seem to keep warm even though the temp is up...fractionally. You look great...work going well?"

"It's going. Your brother is driving us hard...from Israel. Can you believe it? But I don't think you asked me to lunch to talk about Marshall. What's this about two dinner dates? You sounded weird. If I had two men to even talk about, I'd be ecstatic."

The waitress set the sandwiches and coffees on the table, then bustled to a man waving to get her attention.

"Susan, two days ago I had a dinner date, at least I think it was a date...definitely a date, with Charlie Wurthy. I told you about him—grandson of the Chinese man who bought the condo. Thanks again for your help. Charlie said the furnishings, especially the accessories, sold his grandfather."

"And this Charlie is tall, dark, and handsome?"

"You could say that. Then last night I had a dinner date, no, this was more of a business meeting that turned hot."

"Ooo, do go on," Susan said, grinning in anticipation.

"Well, at first I was annoyed. I mean he practically commanded me to meet him for dinner, and he didn't even offer to pick me up."

"Oh, no. Did Charlie pick you up?"

"Yes, in an Uber. Very polite. A consummate gentleman."

"Cold polite or thoughtful polite."

"Warm and thoughtful." Jeli sighed, her finger tracing the rim of her coffee mug. She looked up, her eyes on Susan's. "Very warm."

"Okay, but not hot...as in hot business meeting."

"Definitely different. Because last night...well, last night was quite a rush. Josh was overwhelming with excitement. He's very ambitious, and in a matter of minutes had laid out a plan for the next five years, developing the rest of the condos in the current building, then the whole street, and then developments in other states."

"Umm. Sounds like all business to me. Not—"

"He took my hands, told me he'd put diamonds on my fingers—"

"Whoa. That's maybe too—"

"He took me home, and at the door he kissed me…took my breath away, Susan."

"And the problem is?"

"I'm falling in love with two men."

"Hey, hold on a minute. A couple of dinner dates is not love…not even a fling. Infatuation…maybe," Susan said, leaning against the booth's worn red leatherette.

"Soo?" Jeli fixed her eyes on Susan.

"Sooo, what?"

"So, what do I do?" Jeli asked leaning forward, looking for an answer from her friend, now a best friend forever. She had just shared some intimate thoughts with her BFF.

"Take it slow, Jeli. Enjoy their company. It's way too soon to worry about a date being anything more than dinner."

Jeli's body uncoiled, releasing the tension. Sighing, she leaned back, a smile crossing her face. "How much do I owe you for this most productive therapy session?"

"Next time you can buy the tuna sandwiches."

"Okay. If you want to come with me when I visit Mr. Wu after he moves in, I'll buy you lunch. Of course, I really owe you more than lunch after your help with Faye Yoon."

"By the way, has Marshall mentioned anything about when he might return from Israel?" Susan asked.

"He said another week and that was a couple of days ago. With Josh's big plans, I think I'll have to rent a room. Marshall only has one bedroom, and I'd like to spread out a little."

"I have an idea. Why don't you move in with me? My apartment has two bedrooms, and is close to the T."

"Susan, you can't want me underfoot."

"You wouldn't be underfoot. I think it would be fun."

"Fun? I'd love it…on one condition."

"What's that?"

"I share expenses. After all, you don't know...maybe I eat a ton, leave things helter-skelter, and then there'll be the therapy sessions," Jeli said grinning.

"I think I can handle it, and who knows, maybe I'll be the one on the couch next time. If Marshall is coming home in the few days, why don't you move in tomorrow, or the day after? He'll be exhausted."

"Good thinking. Tomorrow, after you're finished with work. I'll bring a bottle of wine."

"And, I'll give you a key."

The two friends sealed the deal, clinking the rims of their coffee mugs. Susan rooted around her shoulder bag, found her spare key and slid it across the table. Jeli pocketed the key, and arm in arm the pair left the café. With a hug, the friends strode off in opposite directions.

Both smiling, both heads held high. Life was good. Nothing like having a plan.

Chapter 24

———

GRAY DAWN SLID ACROSS the Boston sky. Jeli shook off the blanket, the sheets. She had much to do today and first on the list was to pack her things, launder the bedding and towels, run the dishwasher. In general, putting Marshall's condo back in order. To the sloshing tune of the dishwasher, she texted Marshall letting him know the change in her plans. Five minutes later, she had his reply saying dinner on him when he returned. He wanted a full accounting of what had transpired since he left.

At ten-thirty she sent a text to Josh.

10:30
When U want 2 meet re condos? Jeli

10:34
2 days. Talking to contractor. No check yet from Wu. JG

10:40
OK let me know. Jeli

Jeli stared at her cell, waiting to see if he sent a text back. He didn't.

"You're all business again, Mr. Greely. No word of the diamonds you're putting on my fingers," she mumbled.

Taking a last look around, satisfied, she called for an Uber. She rode down the elevator—two suitcases rolling on either side, a large tote over her shoulder with her laptop, another bag swinging from the other shoulder.

The Uber taxi was waiting at the curb, the driver depositing her bags in the trunk. Navigating the downtown traffic amid honks, traffic lights, the driver pulled to a stop in front of Susan's apartment building.

Bags up on the steps, Jeli paid for the lift, at the same time she heard the Saints marching. It was Charlie.

"Hi, Charlie. How are you?"

"Busy. Heard from Grandfather. He's arriving sooner than I thought. I have to help him get settled—telephone, internet stuff. Sorry, but I have to cancel our evening at the Pops. Gotta go."

"But..."

Jeli stood in the sunshine looking at the blank display.

A truck driver blasted his horn, nudging the traffic to get going, the light was green. A normal day in the city.

With a long sigh, Susan's key in hand, Jeli gained entrance, her suitcase bumping into the brick, four-story building. In the foyer, she faced a sign: Elevator out of order.

Frowning at the sign, and frustrated with Charlie's curt call breaking their date, she bumped up three flights of stairs. "Where's a working elevator when you need it," she muttered. "So, Mr. Charles Wurthy, you were a figment of my wild imagination. So much for the warm, friendly...what was it Susan said? Oh, yes, so much for Mr. Handsome. Two handsome men up, two handsome men down—you're back to zero, Jeli-bean."

Chapter 25

———

NEWS ALERT
Chinese Stock Market
February 2016

———

Following The January selloff, Shanghai Composite falling 6.9%, the following U.S. stocks were particularly hard hit: Netflix fell by 6%, Alphabet down 3.9%, and Facebook down 3.9%.

So far this February, Chinese markets remain volatile with mixed data.

Chapter 26

———

ANOTHER WEEK PASSED BEFORE Jeli finally heard from Charlie. Well, not exactly heard. He sent another text that his grandfather had returned and he and his caregiver were happily ensconced in his new condo. Jeli hadn't heard a peep from Josh that the sale had gone through, but she assumed it had or why would Mr. Wu have taken up residence.

It was Saturday and Susan said she would love to accompany her to visit Wu. Susan was eager to see how all the pieces from Yoon's Furniture looked together.

With a tick up in her spirits, Jeli decided on a new tack—exercise—resolving to rack up ten-thousand steps a day on her step-counter attached to the waist of her new jeans. She cajoled Susan to climb the three flights of stairs to Mr. Wu's condo. Puffing on the fourth-floor landing, leaning against the wall next to the elevator door to catch their breath, the girls laughed, promising more stairs in the future—they were definitely out of condition. Their shape was a non-issue, both had curves.

Jeli knocked on the door and was surprised when it swung open. She raised her brows to Susan.

Why wasn't the door latched or locked?

Peeking through the open doorway, Jeli called out in a soft voice. "Hello…Mr. Wu? Ms. Bradley here, with a friend…welcoming you to your new home." Hesitating, she paused in the doorway listening for a reply. "Susan, let's take off our sneakers. I don't want to leave a mark on the new floors."

"Good idea," Susan said, as she pressed toe to heel of each shoe, lined her sneakers up by Jeli's in the hallway.

With a baby bamboo plant in hand, Jeli stepped to the kitchen island in her sock feet. "Ouch."

"What's the matter?" Susan said.

"I stepped on something," Jeli said, placing the plant on the counter, then stooped over rubbing the bottom of her right foot.

Both girls looked into the living room. Chang-ying's birdcage was covered, centered on the coffee table. Jeli glanced around, took a step back, grabbing Susan's arm.

"Susan...look...the wheelchair is tipped over... by the bay window...Wu's not there. Where..." She whirled around, glanced down. She had stepped on a chess piece. She pointed to the floor. "Look, the chessboard fell off the counter. The pieces are scattered around the barstools."

"Maybe he's taking a nap in the bedroom," Susan said, stepping into the living room.

"Hello, Mr. Qiáng." This time Jeli's voice was raised, commanding. "Are you here?"

"Who's Mr. Qiáng?" Susan asked.

"He's Mr. Wu's companion. He lives with him. He's always by his side. I'll look in the bedroom."

Jeli started toward the bedroom she had so carefully designed for Mr. Wu. She stopped in her tracks, falling to her knees. "Oh, my God. Susan, come here. Mr. Wu...he's on the floor. Hurry," she shouted. Jeli knelt by Wu's side. He was lying face down on the hardwood floor.

"He must have fainted. Help me roll him over."

Susan knelt next to Jeli, her hand on Wu's arm as they turned him over.

Jeli felt for a pulse. "He's not breathing." Wu's eyes were wide open, staring at her.

"Jeli, his arm's cold...I think he's dead."

"Oh my God. Oh my God, Susan...I have to call Charlie."

Still in her parka, Jeli sprang to her feet, ran back to the hallway, to her shoulder bag leaning against her sneakers. Snatching the bag, she rooted around to find her cell. Her hand shaking, she dropped it on the floor.

Picking up her cell, she scrolled the directory for Charlie's number she stored when he had first called her. Tapped the entry.

"Jeli, I'm—"

"Charlie, I'm at your grandfather's condo," she said, gulping for air.

"What's the matter? You sound—"

"Charlie you have to come. Hurry."

"I can't. I'm preparing a presentation for—"

"Charlie...your grandfather's dead."

Chapter 27

———

"CHARLIE'S ON HIS WAY." It was a simple statement. Almost a whisper, Jeli's breathing slightly elevated. She closed the front door, returned to the living room. "I don't know what to do."

"Let's sit down…maybe on the floor. I don't think we should move anything. Let Charlie see the rooms…and the body…as we found them," Susan said.

"That's good. What about Chang-ying, Wu's parrot? He must be asleep. They're trained to rest when the cover is over their cage…he hasn't said a word. He always says hello. Mr. Wu taught him my name…not when he's covered…supposedly. The cage is pretty, gold. Gold cage…imagine that."

"I'm sure it's not real gold, Jeli."

"Probably not."

The pearl-gray walls had turned cold—a cement crypt.

Jeli looked at her watch. Thirty-three or so minutes had passed, when she heard the ding of the elevator, heard the front door open.

"Jeli?"

It was Charlie.

"In here…the living room," Jeli said, as she and Susan got to their feet.

Charlie rounded the corner. Another man entered behind him.

"Where…" He paused seeing the woman standing beside Jeli.

"Charlie, this is my friend Susan Li. Remember? I told you she helped with the furniture selection for—"

Charlie cut her off, turned to the man standing beside him. "Dr. Acker, this is Anjelica Bradley. She called me…and Ms. Li. Where's my grandfather?" Charlie sought Jeli's eyes.

Jeli nodded at the bedroom door. "There…in the doorway."

Charlie hurried to the bedroom, the doctor following.

"Good God. Grandfather. Grandfather." Charlie knelt by his grandfather's side, bending over his lifeless body, gently shaking his shoulders.

Dr. Acker squatted by the body, pressed his fingers to the man's neck feeling for a pulse.

"Charlie, he's gone. He's cold, rigor mortis is setting in—maybe two hours," Acker said.

Charlie looked up at Jeli. "Where's Qiáng?" he snapped. "Did you move Grandfather? How did he get here…the chair—"

"The only thing Susan and I did was roll him onto his back. We thought he was alive. I don't know where Qiáng is. I called you. I don't know how your grandfather got to the bedroom. This is where we found him." Jeli backed away from the bedroom door to Susan, who grasped her hand.

Jeli's mind was a jumble—frightened at seeing Wu's body, the doctor's pronouncement of rigor mortis, startled at Charlie's accusatory tone, like he thought she was responsible.

There was a knock on the front door. The door swung open. Jeli heard footsteps. A man rounded the corner.

It was Josh.

He stared at her. His face changed from a lack of expression to anger. "Where is he? Where's Wu?"

"Josh, he's—"

"What are you doing here?" Charlie said, barring the door into the bedroom, blocking the way to the body.

"I have business being here. Your grandfather's check bounced. I'm looking for cash—"

"Cash! You think he's walking around carrying that kind of cash?"

"Charlie, calm down," the doctor said. "I'm going to call the police. I'm not sure how he died, but it looks as if he hit his head or had a blow to the head. The coroner will tell us the cause of death."

Charlie whirled on the doctor. "Cause of death? I hardly think that's necessary, Dr. Acker. It's obvious he fell, hit his head on…I don't know...the brick fireplace," Charlie said, his eyes snapping from the tipped wheelchair, to the fireplace, to the doctor who was on his cell.

"Maybe that would be a good idea...the police, given the—" Susan began to say, but stopped when Charlie glared at her.

"Charlie, the police are on their way," Acker said.

"Hello, hello," a male voice boomed from the open front door.

"What the hell?" Josh turned, "What are you doing here?"

"It seems the police called the wrong Greely, Josh. Seems they thought I was the owner of this building...where a dead man was found, *son*."

The elevator pinged, door slid open, and a man appeared in the doorway. "Charlie, where are you?" The man glanced at the people assembled in front of him, then walked to Charlie. "What's going on, son? You called that there was something wrong, but you hung up before I could ask what it was about. Where's your grandfather?"

"In the bedroom, Dad."

The ding of the elevator sounded through the open front door, followed by the sound of feet running. A uniformed officer led the way, then medics pulling a gurney. The feet stopped, eyes scanned the array of people. "Where's Dr. Acker?" the lead man said.

"Here. I'm Dr. Acker."

"I'm Detective Shoe and my partner Officer Stewart. You called...a man was found dead?"

"Yes. Over there," Acker nodded his head toward the bedroom door.

"Okay, we see him." The medics scurried to the bedroom, hauling the gurney.

"Do you know the name of the deceased?" Shoe asked the doctor.

"Yes. His name is Mr. Wu. I accompanied Mr. Charles Wurthy here," Dr. Acker said. "He received a call that his grandfather was dead. Charles notified his father, Mr. Stan Wurthy, that Mr. Wu had died. Charles Wurthy is Mr. Wu's grandson."

Another rap on the front door, Faye Yoon walked in, rounded the corner, took one look at the group and made a hasty retreat.

"Faye, wait," Jeli called out, catching up to her, taking hold of her arm. "Faye, something awful has happened. Mr. Wu is dead."

Faye whirled around, her eyes reflecting disbelief. "No, it can't be." Her breathing was labored, searching behind Jeli. "Charlie?"

"Yes, Charlie's here, but..." Jeli followed Faye's line of sight, turned back to Faye. "He's talking to the doctor."

"Excuse me," Faye Yoon said, making a beeline for the door, clip-clopping on her high heels to the stairs, ignoring the elevator.

Detective Shoe raced after her. "Wait. What's your name?"

"Faye Yoon. Ask the woman in the parka."

The officer wrote the name on his pad, turned back inside the condo.

Everyone turned to the door at the ding of the elevator. Qiáng stepped out. At the sight of the uniformed officer, he dropped the bags of groceries in his arms, oranges rolling on the floor from Qiáng to the officer's feet.

Chapter 28

———

THE MEDICS ROLLED THE gurney out of the bedroom carrying Mr. Wu in a black body bag. No one spoke, stepping back to allow an alley way, eyes following the gurney to the front door. The medics paused, allowing Qiáng to retrieve the oranges.

The elevator door opened accepting the passengers, and closed.

Everyone spoke at once.

"Hold it! Everybody, please take a seat and don't touch anything. I need your names, telephone numbers, and how you knew the deceased. Then you can leave."

Joshua Greely, standing next to his son, shook his head then stepped to the officer, giving him his name, and telephone number along with his business card. The detective asked how he knew the deceased.

"Never met him. My son owns the building. Anything else you want to know, ask my son. If anything requires clarification, you can contact me at the number on the card," Greely said and left taking the stairs.

"And you, sir. Your name?" Shoe said turning to the burly Chinaman.

"Billy Qiáng. What happened? Who was that...on the stretcher?"

"The deceased is Mr. Wu. What brings you here today?" Shoe asked.

"What? No." Billy ran to the elevator, turned back to the detective, shaking his head in shocked disbelief. "I'm Mr. Wu's caregiver, but I don't understand. We were just moving in...excuse me, excuse me, I have groceries to put away," Qiáng whispered, his shoulders drooping as he made his way to the kitchen putting the grocery bags on the counter by the refrigerator.

Jeli rushed to his side.

"Ms. Bradley...I can't breathe."

Qiáng slid down the refrigerator to the floor, legs splayed out in front of him.

Jeli opened a cabinet, slammed it shut. Finding glasses in the next cabinet, she added tap water and handed it to Qiáng, holding it to his lips. "Drink, Mr. Qiáng, it will help settle you," she said squatting next to him. "You'll be okay. Can I call you Billy?

"Help me," Billy gasped.

Jeli nodded. She stood, her eyes sweeping the room.

Detective Shoe turned to the doctor just as there was a faint knock on the open door. Perfume preceded Quin Shi as she stepped inside, looked at Josh. "What's going on?"

"Seems Mr. Wu is dead," Josh said, turning his head away from her strong scent.

"No. How awful. Heart attack?" she said, her fingers covering her mouth.

"What's your name, Ms.—"

"Quin Shi. I'm a realtor. Mr. Wu was my client. Josh—"

"Please spell your name...do you have a business card?"

"Yes, of course." Quin Shi retrieved a card from her purse, handed it to the officer. She looked at Josh. "Josh, call me when you can." Turning, she left, taking the elevator down to the front entrance.

"Okay, you two. Names please," the detective said looking at Susan, then Jeli behind the island as she helped Qiáng to his feet.

The two women gave him their names and cell numbers.

"Jeli, I'll see you back at the apartment...unless you want to come with me now?" Susan said.

"No, you go ahead," Jeli said, guiding Billy to the couch.

Stan Wurthy walked into the bedroom.

"Don't touch anything, sir," Shoe called out.

"I won't, I won't."

Shoe turned back, looking at Charlie. "Okay, your name is Charles Wurthy the doctor said. You're the grandson of the deceased?"

"Yes. My mother was Mr. Wu's daughter," Charlie said.

Your number please, and address," Shoe said

"Here's my business card."

"Good. Good. And you, sir, your name," Shoe said, pen poised over his notepad, looking at Josh.

"Josh Greely. You met my father, Joshua Greely. I'm a developer. Here's my card. I own the building. Mr. Wu bought this condo from me, but he stiffed me," Josh's said raising his voice. "His check bounced. If that's it, I'll be going, and you, Qiáng," he shouted, "get out. Take the sacks of whatever you bought and get out."

Jeli laid her hand on Josh's arm. "Josh, let him stay, at least for a few nights. He just lost the man he was caring for. He has no place to go...no family."

Josh jerked away. "Okay, three nights...then out. If you're done with me, Detective, I'll be leaving," Josh said, yanking up the zipper on his coat.

"You can leave, sir. I will be in touch later...with you owning the building, I'm sure there'll be questions."

"Come on, Red, let's get out of here," Josh said.

"Not yet, miss. You found the body?"

"Yes. I decorated this condo for Mr. Wu, and I asked Susan Li to come with me to welcome him to his new home. That was the only reason Susan was here."

"Don't leave, Ms. Bradley. I need your statement—tell me exactly what you found. Mr. Greely, you may go."

Josh glared at Jeli, then bolted out the door, his western boots banging down the stairs.

Shoe turned to Stan and Charles Wurthy. "I'm sorry for your loss—your father-in-law, Mr. Wurthy, and you, Charles, for your grandfather. I'd like you to have a seat. I have a few questions, but first, Ms. Bradley, I'd like you to walk around the condo with me. Tell me exactly what you saw when you entered, and particularly, seeing how you designed the rooms, what is different—new or missing."

Chapter 29

———

DETECTIVE SHOE STOOD AT the bay window watching his partner retrieve evidence bags and a camera from the trunk of the squad car.

Jeli stood near the kitchen island, Charlie sat on the couch, both waiting for Officer Stewart so they could get on with the investigation and leave. Charlie was obviously struggling—pacing to the fireplace, then again sitting on the couch.

With the ding of the elevator, Officer Stewart emerged with the equipment to capture anything he and Detective Shoe might find to develop the story the condo held secret.

Snapping on white poly-gloves to prevent any chance of compromising the evidence, Detective Shoe glanced around, his eyes coming to rest on Jeli.

"Let's start in the kitchen, Ms. Bradley. Anything amiss?"

Standing by the sink, Jeli shook her head.

Charlie leaned against the island watching her.

"Okay, let's step to the other side of the island. Now, do you see anything out of place, or missing?"

"Yes, several things, the chessboard for one. When I was here last, the board was on the island. It's now on the floor...pieces are scattered. In fact, when I walked in with Susan, I had taken off my sneakers and hurt my foot when I stepped on a piece."

"Very good, Ms. Bradley, exactly what I want—no embellishments, just the facts." Shoe nodded to the officer to bag the chessboard and the pieces on the floor. Jeli stooped to pick up a piece but Shoe warned her not to touch anything. "We don't want to add your fingerprints to the mix, Ms. Bradley."

"You may find my fingerprint on one or two pieces from when Mr. Wu explained them...the difference between Chinese chess pieces and the sets that are sold in the States."

"Go on, Ms. Bradley—what else do you see?"

"The wheelchair was tipped over and, of course, Mr. Wu was found in the bedroom doorway. To my knowledge he couldn't walk, so I don't—"

"Anything else?" Shoe asked.

Jeli glanced around, arms crossed over her chest. "No, everything seems to be as I remember."

"Okay, let's go into the bedroom."

Officer Stewart took pictures of the wheelchair and followed in line behind the others and Charlie.

Detective Shoe glanced around and once again addressed Jeli. "The medics, who retrieved the body, taped an outline of the deceased as they found him. Is it as you found him, Ms. Bradley?"

"Pretty much, except the tape is more in the shape *after* Susan and I rolled Mr. Wu on his back. I thought he was alive...maybe just passed out. But sadly that was not the case."

"The chest of drawers, the chair?"

"Nothing appears disturbed," Jeli said, her eyes sweeping the room.

Stewart took pictures of the body's taped outline.

"Please check the bathroom. Tell me if you see anything out of place."

Jeli entered the bathroom and returned.

"Nothing, Detective."

"Okay, I saw a second bedroom. Let's have a look."

"That was to be Mr. Qiáng's room. I believe he retreated there after Josh Greely left."

"It's okay, Ms. Bradley. Let's go in." Shoe rapped on the door and opened it.

Qiáng was standing by the window. He turned his back to the detective and the others, stared out the window. Jeli thought he looked frightened, as he did when he dropped the groceries in the front doorway, but he seemed to have regained his composure.

"Mr. Qiáng, when I've finished the walk through with Ms. Bradley, I will do the same with you. Do not leave. Do you understand?"

The muscular man nodded his head, but didn't move, continuing to stare out the window.

"Ms. Bradley?"

"Everything is as I had positioned it."

Shoe led the procession out of Qiáng's bedroom, returning to the living room. Officer Stewart closed Qiáng's bedroom door as he left, leaving Qiáng to stare out the window.

"Ms. Bradley—"

"There's one more thing, Detective. Chang-ying, Mr. Wu's parrot talks. Says 'hello' and 'bye.' But as you can see the cage is covered—good thing or he'd be very agitated—so many visitors..."

Shoe stepped to the covered cage sitting on the coffee table, pulled off the cover. Jeli gasped, her hand covering her mouth. Chang-ying was lying on the bottom of the cage. Dead.

The group stared down at the lifeless parrot.

"Detective Shoe, there's a chess piece in the corner of the cage, in the food cup," Jeli said.

Without taking his eyes from the parrot, Shoe directed his officer to take pictures of the cage—placement on the table, close-up of the bird, of the food cup, and closer still of the chess piece. Shoe asked his partner to replace the cover, and to carefully transport the cage to the lab for analysis—the bird, and the food. "I want to know what killed the parrot. Today if possible. Ms. Bradley and Mr. Wurthy, that will be all for now. Needless to say, I'm sure I will have more questions. Mr. Wurthy, I'll contact you tomorrow for your full statement—for the record."

Chapter 30

———

AS SUDDENLY AS THE gaggle of people who had a connection to Mr. Wu congregated along with Detective Shoe and Officer Stewart, they just as suddenly dissipated. Qiáng remained in his room behind the closed door. Charlie and Jeli were left standing, staring at each other.

Charlie slumped on the couch, facing the fireplace, a few seeds of parrot food on the coffee table in between. Jeli sat on a side chair, leaning forward, hands clasped, worry creases across her forehead. She didn't know what to say but had to give a try at comforting him.

"Charlie, I'm so sorry…all your plans…together again after so many years."

Charlie shook his head. In slow motion, he got to his feet, ambled to the bay window. The sun was setting behind thickening clouds, leaving the trees in dark silhouette, the snow banks a dirty gray.

"Let's get out of here, Anjelica. I'm suddenly very hungry. Can you…join me for dinner?" His words said in a muffled whisper.

"Of course. I'll let Qiáng know we're leaving. Poor Qiáng…unless you—"

"No. I don't want to be with anyone else…maybe tomorrow."

———

THE BLACK NIGHT OF evening crept over Boston. Charlie paid the Uber driver then took Jeli's hand, helping her navigate the icy walkway to the front door of one of the many bars in the Beacon Hill area with a fireplace.

Nightlife in the city had yet to begin. The bar was cozy but didn't seem to soothe Charlie's mood. The warmth did, as he held Jeli's hand leading her to a table near the fireplace.

A waitress approached, smiled. "Cocktails?"

"Yes, please. I'd like a scotch, rocks on the side. Anjelica?"

Jeli thought of Gran—when times were calm, all right with the world, she'd light up a cigarillo along with a scotch on the rocks. If everything was in chaos, she skipped the cigarillo and went for the scotch.

"Make that two, please," Jeli said.

Charlie didn't react to her order, or didn't hear. He was staring into the fire.

"My father, Stan Wurthy, met Amy Wu on a trip to China. He was taking a sabbatical from his Masters in Business Finance at Harvard. Mr. Wu was Amy's father and very much against her getting married. To make matters worse, Amy became pregnant with me. Grandfather counseled her to go to America to have the baby so the child would have dual citizenship."

The waitress came with their drinks. Charlie waved her off— they would order dinner later.

Jeli listened, watched Charlie as he rambled on about his mother. He stopped for a sip of his drink, then continued.

"My mother was seven months pregnant, I'm told, and wanted to wear a proper wedding dress so they waited to get married. She came to the States, stayed with my father. She returned to Beijing within a month after I was born. My father, you met him today—Stan Wurthy—traveled extensively in China, quickly establishing himself as a liaison to the developing Chinese stock market, becoming a stockbroker. Being an American gave great credence to his market expertise. He became very wealthy."

Charlie abruptly stood, took a step to the fireplace.

Jeli could see he was troubled about something.

"Wait, wait. Backup. Way before his success...when he was building his business in China—"

The waitress returned. Charlie ordered another round of drinks and two burgers to go, in separate containers.

"My grandmother kept pushing my mother to get married and so they set a date. No, that's not right...yes, it is, but that was before...no, after I was born...when my mother returned to China they set a date. The afternoon the wedding was to take place, there was a terrible car accident. My grandfather was driving with my grandmother and my mother. My father was going to meet them.

"As my grandfather told me, when I was old enough to understand, the traffic was horrendous. Many Chinese were doing everything they could to escape the poverty on the farm, hoping to make a better life, find a job in the city. There were many stories my grandfather told me about enticing the farmers to the city—the city became clogged with farmers."

Jeli sat mesmerized. His story was choppy, bits and pieces out of order.

The second round of drinks was set on the table, along with two white foam containers. The waitress set the check on the table and left.

Charlie continued to stare into the flames. He picked up his drink, took a long swallow.

"As I said, there was a car accident. The car that grandfather was driving was hit broadside, causing it to careen into another car. A third car hit the skidding car. My grandmother and my mother were killed, and grandfather was left a cripple. There was a settlement—awarding my grandfather with enough money to leave the farm and move to the city. It was enough to buy a cleaning business."

"How old were you?" Jeli asked.

"Six months. I was left that day with a neighboring farmer's wife."

Charlie laid his hand over Jeli's. "I'm sorry. I thought I was hungry, but...I can't stomach the thought of food. I'll take you home. I hope you understand."

"I do understand, but call me tomorrow or whenever if you want to talk."

"I will, and thank you."

The evening drew to a close. In the back of the Uber Jeli glanced at Charlie staring out the window, his profile highlighted now and again by a street lamp, tears streaming down his face.

Chapter 31

THE APARTMENT WAS DARK except for the soft glow of the small table lamp in the living room. Jeli stood a moment letting the warmth of the room envelop her in a quiet cocoon. Her shoulders slumped, a small breath of air escaping her lips.

It had been twelve hours since she and Susan had left the apartment on their way to welcome Mr. Wu to his new home. Twelve hours since finding his body and witnessing all of the chaos that ensued.

She slipped off her sneakers, tiptoed in, setting her tote on the floor next to the couch. Padding to the refrigerator, she put the foam container with the burger on the shelf, then tiptoed to her room. After changing into a pair of comfy blue flannel pajamas, she decided a mug of hot chocolate might be the ticket to help her block out the day's drama. Learning that Wu's check had bounced, she faced the prospect of searching for a new job.

"Hey, girlfriend, are you okay?" Susan said, tying the belt of her fuzzy bathrobe, yawning, rubbing her eyes. "Cup a cocoa?"

"You read my mind. With marshmallows if you have some," Jeli said.

"I do. Go curl up on the couch. I'll take care of the cocoa." Susan heated the milk, stirred in the cocoa powder, and added a few drops of vanilla flavoring. Topping the mugs with marshmallows, she handed Jeli a mug and then snuggled into her lounger.

"So, tell me what happened after I left."

Jeli took a tentative sip of the hot cocoa, wiping away a dab of marshmallow on her upper lip.

"Bullet points are as follows. Medics carted Mr. Wu's body off to the morgue. The coroner will determine cause of death.

Detective Shoe is making arrangements to take a for-the-record statement from everyone who showed up at the condo—probably starting tomorrow. Oh, the parrot died. You saw the birdcage. When the detective removed the cover, there was poor Chang-ying. Oh, and Charlie took me out for drinks, which turned into dinner, which turned into takeout. There's a burger in the fridge."

Sipping the cocoa, Jeli looked over at Susan.

"He's crushed, Susan. Charlie told me about his family—a tragic story. His mother was killed in a car crash when he was six months old, his grandmother killed in the same accident, which also left his grandfather a cripple. So his entire maternal side of the family is gone, leaving only his father. Susan, he was crying—just sitting in the Uber taxi beside me...crying."

"What did you say?"

"What could I say...only that I was sorry for his loss. I felt so helpless."

"You were there, Jeli. You were with him and that's what he needed most, to know he wasn't alone."

"I guess so."

"That's tough. He instinctively reached out to you for comfort—what about his father? He was Wu's son-in-law."

"There's no significance to his asking me out. I was there, and I think he just wanted to talk. His father left soon after you did. I didn't have a chance to talk to him."

"Jeli, the whole thing was so strange."

"I know."

"You and I, then within a matter of...well, less than an hour, all those people arrived. Did you know them?" Susan asked.

"I didn't know them, but I knew who they were...except for Charlie's father. I'd never seen him before."

"Umm. So strange."

"Susan, the strangest thing of all, well, except for the dead parrot, how did Wu get from his wheelchair to the bedroom—walk? Crawl...dragged? But if he was dragged...no, no way...unless Qiáng was faking surprise, faking shock...faking..."

"Do you think he could have killed Mr. Wu? Is that what you're thinking?" Susan's words, a whisper, hung in the air.

"Murder? No. Mr. Wu was a sweet old man. He probably fell out of his chair and tried to get...tried to get to the bedroom telephone to call for help. The exertion from crawling... I bet the coroner will find it was a heart attack. Murder is out of the question. There's no reason."

A frown under furrowed brows crossed Jeli's face.

"What's wrong?" Susan asked.

"Something, but I can't put my finger on it. Wu lying on the floor. When the doctor was checking him, tried to raise his hand, his arm was already a little stiff...wait...now, I remember. Mr. Wu wore a big gold band with a diamond when he arrived the first day to look at the condo. Josh and I commented on it. Josh thought the ring must have been worth lots of money."

"So?" Susan said.

"So, I just realized he wasn't wearing the ring when the doc picked up his hand."

"Maybe he didn't wear it all the time."

"Maybe, but still..."

Jeli took their empty mugs to the kitchen sink. "I'm heading to bed." Jeli paused. "Susan, thank you for coming with me this morning. As things turned out, your being there helped more than you know. I owe you one. Night."

Chapter 32

———

MONDAY, TWO DAYS SINCE Jeli and Susan found Mr. Wu's body in the doorway to his bedroom. The coroner left word for Detective Shoe, that his report would be completed by tomorrow. Jeli received a call from the detective just after breakfast requesting that she come to the condo at noon. He planned to begin taking statements from everyone on his list compiled on Saturday from the drop-ins, as he called them. He was starting with her and Billy Qiáng. He was particularly eager that she join Qiáng's interview.

At five minutes to eleven, Jeli pressed the buzzer at the street entrance and was immediately buzzed in. Riding the elevator, Jeli straightened her tan car coat, pulled the belt tight. Although Shoe hadn't said anything about Josh on the telephone, she hoped she might see him and wanted to present a professional image, keeping her in his mind for future jobs. The sidewalks around the city were dry—the heels of the fashion boot didn't give her a problem. It was still cold, so she bundled up in a black turtleneck layered under a rich, dark green vest over black wool slacks. She had teased her hair into a bonfire of red curls.

Stepping off the elevator, she was greeted by the detective.

"Ms. Bradley, thank you for coming. We're in the living room."

Jeli nodded to Qiáng, then sat on a chair next to the fireplace. She noted that the wheelchair was upright by the bay window.

"As I was saying, Mr. Qiáng, how long have you known Mr. Wu?"

"Two years."

"And how was it Mr. Wu hired you as...as...what did you actually do for Mr. Wu?"

"I was his companion. Some people called me a caregiver."

"How did you happen to be given that job?"

"He owned a laundry...I met him at the laundry."

"You were picking up your laundry?"

"Not exactly."

"Then how, exactly, did he happen to hire you?"

Qiáng looked out the window, then his head bent forward, hands on his knees. "He caught me with my fingers in the cash box. He yelled at me, started dialing. I knew he was calling the police. But he hung up...didn't complete the call. He ordered me to sit down. He started talking to me...talking in a quiet voice, asked me why I was trying to steal his money."

Qiáng's right heel began bouncing on the red Oriental rug.

"I told him I lost my job. A bunch of us were fired. Money dried up." Qiáng rubbed his knees. He began to sweat, swiped at his brow with the sleeve of his black flannel shirt. "I was hungry. I hadn't eaten for a couple of days. Mr. Wu said he needed somebody because his companion had moved away. He said he'd give me a week's trial if I wanted. That was two years ago."

"Mr. Wu was a cripple. His needs must have been extensive. Did you get any time off?"

"Oh, yes sir—every day. Usually when I ran errands for him, but I never stayed away long, less than an hour. He could handle the laundry business, short spurts, unless a customer was unhappy with his cleaning, or there was a mix up. He'd call me on my cell if he needed me quick like."

"Your English is good. How is that?"

"It was a reason he hired me. My mother taught English to workers in shops where English-speaking tourists frequented. She was a teacher in a Chinese school, so, while English is hard, she mastered it, and said I had to learn too. That it would be helpful someday. Anyway, at home, Beijing, I took Mr. Wu to the gym, or I'd go for groceries when he was napping—he'd close the shop for an hour every afternoon."

"He paid you well?"

"Well enough—room and board, a weekly allowance."

"Now, what are you going to do, Billy? May I call you Billy?"

"Sure. Those who know me call me Billy. I guess I'll go back to China. I don't know."

"I'm still amazed at how well you speak English," Shoe said.

"I was a mail guy for an American company. My boss paid for me to take English, adding to what my mother had taught me. Then I was a delivery guy, working my way up. But things changed. Things changed over the last five years especially in Beijing. Chinese companies were going under because the stock market was crashing. They had extended themselves, too much debt. I don't know how all that works, but Mr. Wu did."

"Was Mr. Wu good to you?"

"Yes sir, except when money was short. I guess after the accident, I didn't know him then, he received a settlement...from the accident, I think. He never really talked about it. That's when he opened the laundry—boom or bust—but somehow he always kept afloat until the past month. He played the market. He moaned how he lost everything but he had already bought the tickets for us to come to the States, to Boston."

"I see. Tell me what you did Saturday morning before you returned from grocery shopping."

"I fixed Mr. Wu his breakfast, helped him shower. He said he was going to nap in his chair and for me to go along. That's it, until I got off the elevator with the grocery bags."

"Billy, could Mr. Wu walk?"

"No. Never. Stand, holding on to me, yes, so I could help him dress. His arms were strong...worked out at the gym, as I said."

"He never walked in your presence?"

"Never."

"Thank you, Billy. I think that's it for now."

Billy stood, nodded to Jeli and strolled back to his room, shutting the door.

Shoe reached in his pants pocket, drawing out his cell. He walked to the window, his back to Jeli, as he conversed with the caller. Thanking the caller, he shut his cell and turned to Jeli.

"The coroner's report just came in. We'll have to postpone your statement...maybe tomorrow?"

"OK, but I don't have anything to add to what I told you before. But I'd be happy to help any way I can."

"Would you like me to drop you off...unless you have a car?"

"No car, but thanks for the offer anyway. Have you ever been to China, Detective?"

"No, I haven't. You?"

"No. I've never been out of New England, but I'd like to. Maybe if Mr. Greely comes through with more clients, and I save...I mean really save, then China is going to be on the top of my list. You know, with Billy being bilingual and all, I think I'll talk to my brother about hiring him. He might have a spot for him."

Jeli and the detective rode the elevator down and parted in different directions—the detective in his squad car, Jeli deep in thought about Billy, Mr. Wu, China and then switching to Susan— maybe another hot cocoa night. Her head went up a notch, strides lengthened. "I'm going to travel. I'm going to China!" she said, passing some kids in the street laughing, throwing snowballs.

Chapter 33

———

THE CORONER'S REPORT WAS IN.

Given the contents of the report, Detective Shoe requested Stan Wurthy and his son Charles meet him at the condo this morning along with Ms. Bradley. He wanted to go over her statement, being as she found the body, but he also deemed her presence essential, given her keen sense of observation. The report contained a bombshell and he wanted everyone close to Mr. Wu, including Billy Qiáng, to be present to see their reaction to the report. Shoe also requested Officer Stewart, who had bagged the evidence, to be in attendance.

Everyone was seated in the living room. Wu's wheelchair was positioned near the fireplace, the place where Jeli found it tipped over the day Wu met his end.

Shuffling the papers in the file folder he held, Shoe stood at the fireplace, at the opposite side of the wheelchair. Satisfied the documents were in the proper order, he faced the group.

Jeli was sitting on a side chair between the wheelchair and the couch. She had a creepy feeling that Mr. Wu was sitting in his wheelchair beside her, watching everyone.

"Since the morning of Mr. Wu's death, my partner and I pondered how Mr. Wu died. One explanation, given the wheelchair was tipped on its side, was that Mr. Wu had fallen, hit his head on the brick hearth here," Shoe paused, pointed to the bricks, then looked from one to the other of the four sitting in front of him. He picked up the top sheet of paper, waved it at those assembled, then placed it back under his thumb.

"The report reads that Mr. Wu did in fact suffer a blow to the head, the back of his head. Umm, he would have fallen backward, not forward out of his chair. So the theory that he hit his head on the hearth doesn't fit. The coroner believes the blow to his head was caused by a blunt instrument. The approximate time of death is believed to be sometime between 8:00 and 10:00 a.m. Ms. Bradley found the body at 10:30 a.m."

Shoe paused, took a breath, and continued. "It appears Mr. Wu was murdered."

The sound of everyone sucking up air at Shoe's uttering the word murder, punctuated his statement.

"It would be impossible for him to have hit himself over the head with enough force to cause his death. Or, that a fall, from a sitting position in his wheelchair, even if by some chance he did hit his head on a brick from say a height of less than two feet, would have killed him."

Stan Wurthy stood up, paced to the bay window, looked down at the street. "Detective Shoe, Charlie and I talked about taking care of his grandfather's remains. When can you release the body so we can make the arrangements? Cremation is the norm in China. Charlie wants to cremate his grandfather here as soon as you release the body. Sometime in the next few months, Charlie will travel to Beijing to visit the burial site of his grandmother and mother. It is his desire to scatter the ashes over their graves."

"Because we now have a murder investigation, it will be at least a week," Shoe said. "You can contact the coroner directly. With the time of death established, I have to verify the statements you gave me on Saturday. Billy, you told me that you went out for groceries that morning. What time did you leave and what time did you return, and how was Mr. Wu when you left?"

"I'm not sure when I left but it was around eight o'clock. I remember Mr. Wu had finished his breakfast tray, and I had put the dishes in the dishwasher. He said he was going to read. Most often after he eats he likes to take a nap. After the long trip from Beijing, moving in here, he was still very tired."

"You told me, when you went out, it was usually only for an hour. So, when you're out for more than hour or so, he can fend for himself...the bathroom?"

"Yes, he wheels himself into the bathroom. After we first looked at the condo, he asked me to check with Mr. Greely if it was possible to install an iron bar on either side of the toilet so he could swing from the chair to the toilet," Billy said. "You know when I returned, Detective. You were here. The reason I was gone longer than usual was the rental car. Charlie didn't have a car for our use as yet. Anyway, the rental car had a flat tire...I found it when I finished buying the groceries. So I had to call the rental agency. They swapped cars...I didn't return to the condo until close to eleven. You saw me...when I dropped the groceries, the oranges—"

"Yes, I do remember the oranges," Shoe said.

"Ms. Bradley, you stated that you and your friend, Susan Li, arrived about ten thirty. Is that right?"

"Yes. The door wasn't latched and when I knocked it swung open. I called out, and then I found Mr. Wu in the doorway of the bedroom."

"Yes, about ten feet from the fireplace." Shoe made a note on his pad, then turned to Charlie.

"Charlie, please tell me where you were at eight o'clock that morning."

"I was at work. Anjelica called me...told me how she found my grandfather. I rushed right over."

"And who can verify you were at work?"

"No one. I like to come in early. It's quiet. I usually get in around six thirty, seven on a Saturday. When Anjelica called I raced out, down the emergency staircase."

"So, no one saw you in your office?"

"I guess not."

"And Mr. Wurthy, where were you at eight o'clock that morning?" Shoe said.

"I was in my office. None of my staff was in that day. As Charlie said, it was Saturday."

"And, why were you in the office...Saturday?" Shoe said, his eyes pinched as he looked at Stan Wurthy.

"If you must know, I was preparing bankruptcy documents."

"Dad, you didn't tell me—"

"I was going to, Charlie. I was putting it off, hoping that I could solve the financial situation. I'll discuss it later."

"Ms. Bradley, eight o'clock?" Shoe asked.

"I was with Susan all morning. We left together to welcome Mr. Wu. I'm sharing her apartment for awhile. We arrived here about ten thirty."

"Okay. I guess that wraps it up for now. You're all free to be on your way but please don't leave town. I'm sure there will be more questions. Oh, I would be remiss, if I didn't ask, does anyone have an idea who might want Mr. Wu dead?"

Glances flashed from one to the other, but no one offered a name.

Detective Shoe shuffled the papers again, adjusted his arm length. "If you all have no one to add, then I will be visiting the two who wandered in that morning, a Ms. Faye Yoon, and Ms. Quin Shi. Still no suggestions on who might have wanted Mr. Wu dead? Mr. Qiáng, no one accompanied you from China?"

"No, sir. Charlie arranged our flight. First-class seats, just the two of us. He met us at the airport, took us to his apartment so Mr. Wu could rest."

Everyone stood, began bundling up to leave.

Shoe's brows furrowed. "Oh, I do have one more question. Charlie, did your grandfather have a will?"

"Not that I know of," Charlie said, zipping up his parka.

"Billy, do you know if Mr. Wu had a will?"

"He never said, but I did take him to an appointment with his lawyer just before we left China. I assumed it was about selling or leasing the laundry business. A few days before we left for the States, a farmer friend of his offered to run it. Maybe there was more to it. I don't know anything about the arrangement they had."

"I see."

"I have a question, Detective," Jeli said, pulling on her green mittens.

"And what's that, Ms. Bradley?"

"Chang-ying, Mr. Wu's parrot, what killed him? And, how did Mr. Wu get to the bedroom?"

"A broken neck, Ms. Bradley. The bird died of a broken neck."

"But...?"

"Yes, my questions too. I don't have an answer to either one...yet."

Chapter 34

———

THE SAINTS WERE ON the march. Jeli reached for her phone and grinned at the Caller ID—Travis.

"Hey, Trav. Funny you should call. I was thinking I should give you a jingle."

"Are you all right?"

"Yes and no. I may be out of a job. At least I broke my record, being it was my first real job —kept it for two months. Why are you asking? Did Sadie ask you to check on her baby sis?"

"I received a report from Boston about a Chinese man who died under suspicious circumstances in Boston. Attached to the report was a list of people the detective was gathering statements from. Much to my surprise, make that shock, your name was on the list. Several Chinese names were included and some American men."

"Wow, I made the big leagues. The dead man is a Mr. Wu. I did the interior design for a condo he was buying. The Chinese listed...is one Faye Yoon?"

"Yes, and another is Quin Shi. Do you know them?"

"Faye Yoon helped me pick out the furniture that would be appropriate given the different cultures. I only met Quin Shi once. She's the real estate broker who introduced Mr. Wu to the developer I'm working for, Josh Greely. Does your report say anything about him?"

"Two by the name of Greely, father and son. Seems the Boston Bureau has been watching Quin Shi. The report says Ms. Shi is believed to be a front for a Chinese conglomerate. She could be involved in money laundering—helping Chinese move money out of China, particularly to buy US properties," Travis said.

"Nothing illegal putting a Chinese buyer together with an American seller is there? That can't be considered laundering money can it?" Jeli said.

"No. Her name was highlighted because of her suspicious activities in the real estate market. Jeli, be careful and don't sign any documents unless you talk to me first."

"Roger that. Tell Sadie, hi, and, Travis, thanks for the heads up. Are you and Sadie coming to the farm soon?"

"I can't confirm a date yet, but it looks like we may be able to get away from D.C. for a few days next month. We both need a change of scene."

———

JELI DISCONNECTED THE CALL and immediately tapped in Detective Shoe's number.

"Hi, Detective. Ms. Bradley here."

"I see that. What can I do for you?"

"Well, I was thinking, being as you said I was very observant, and being that I was the interior designer for the property where Mr. Wu was found, I wondered if it would be okay with you if I sat in on your interviews with Quin Shi and Faye Yoon. I could listen, watch, to see if I picked up on any misstatements, being as I'm sort of involved."

"You might be helpful. I'm meeting with both of them tomorrow—Ms. Shi at ten and Ms. Yoon at one. Both of them in their offices."

"I'll be there, Detective. If there's any change in time, give me a buzz. Oops, my brother's calling. See you tomorrow."

"Hey, Marsh, you're back? I've missed you."

"Missed me so much you moved out?"

"I told you...definitely left a note. Susan and I hit it off—like sisters. She offered and I accepted. I was cramping your style—"

"I have no style, but I'm glad to hear it's working out for you two. She's very nice. Are you paying your way?"

"Ugh! Of course, I am. Mr. bossy, bossy, bossy."

"Sadie called," Marshall said. "She asked me to keep an eye on you—"

"Sadie did? Good grief. I just hung up with Trav."

"Well, she said you may be involved in something over your head, and—"

"My God, you two sure channel each other. This twin thing is getting out of hand. Just so you know, my client was murdered. How's that for more info than you needed to know, and don't tell Mom and Pops, or Gran."

"Murdered?"

"Yep big brother, just like your cyber-hacker criminals only different. I'm helping the detective. He thinks I'm observant."

"Jeli, maybe you'd better move back in with me."

"Oh no, and by the way the next time I see you, I was going to suggest someone for your company. He's bilingual—English, Chinese. He's not a programmer, but maybe you could use him somewhere. He needs a job...he was left high and dry when his boss died. His name is Billy Qiáng. Call me if you want his number. Hey, I'm planning on going to the farm this weekend. Can—"

"Can't make it. Learned some stuff from the cyber security company I visited in Tel Aviv that...well, I can't get away. Jeli..."

"Yes?"

"Promise you'll call if you need help. Lunch next week?"

"Sure. Thanks for checking up on me...NOT. I'll try for next week, but there's this fascinating murder case I'm working on. Bye." Jeli giggled, pocketing her phone.

Chapter 35

———

SHOULD SHE OR SHOULDN'T SHE?

Head down, watching for ice, Jeli pondered the question of whether to tell Detective Shoe about her conversation with Travis. Travis didn't say not to relay the information, something he was aware of but wasn't included in the report he received from the Boston bureau—Quin Shi under suspicion of money laundering. Nothing official. But Jeli certainly didn't want to get the FBI agent, her future brother-in-law, in trouble. Deciding she'd learn more if she kept her mouth shut and listened, she pushed open the door to the offices of Quin Shi, Boston Area Real Estate.

Detective Shoe was just hanging his coat on the coat rack. Quin, standing beside him, displayed a hint of surprise, brows arching for a split second over her large black eyes as Jeli walked in.

Shoe caught her look as well. "I believe you know, Ms. Bradley?" he said to Ms. Shi.

"We've met. So nice to see you, Ms. Bradley. Dreadful about poor Mr. Wu. Tea? Let me get another cup."

"Thank you, Ms. Shi," the detective said, settling at a large rosewood conference table to one side of the open office. Opposite was a seating area, chairs and a loveseat around an oval glass coffee table, a basket of greenery placed in the center.

Jeli scanned the area, taking in the ambiance of the space—a relaxing place to negotiate real estate deals over a cup of coffee or tea, a conference table for the signing of purchase and sale documents.

Shoe laid a legal-size yellow pad with green lines on the table as Quin poured tea into three china cups. Sugar and cream were on a silver tray in the center of the table along with small silver spoons and white embossed paper napkins.

Tension bounced between Shi and Shoe, tension that neither acknowledged verbally, only noticeable in their body language—stiff, adversarial.

"So, Ms. Shi, how did you come to know Mr. Wu?"

"Through a liaison in Beijing. We give each other leads. Some leads are for rentals—people traveling for a vacation one way or the other—Boston to Beijing, or Beijing to Boston—sometimes resulting in a jump off to other cities."

"But Mr. Wu was buying property. There must be a lot of red tape in such a transaction—bank accounts to set up, loans to be applied for?" Shoe asked, taking a sip of tea.

Jeli felt like she was watching a ping pong match. *Maybe Shoe already knows about her dirty laundry,* she thought.

"There can be. I do try to facilitate a rental or a sale—the financial aspect, and at times schools for children, and every now and then, help in finding a job if family members require employment. But none of that was the case for Mr. Wu. He was moving to Boston and was considered a family member. His grandson, Charles Wurthy, sponsored him, enabling him to obtain a visa for himself and his caregiver."

Quin Shi sipped her tea, set the cup back on the saucer, and continued to detail her business with her client.

"Mr. Wu paid for the property in cash...was going to pay in cash that is. I only found out...the reason I came to the condo when I gave you my name, found out the night before that his check bounced. Of course, I was furious. I've never had that happen before. The Chinese are very trustworthy and my contact vouches for each buyer he refers to me. My specialty is making deals with those in China who wish to buy property in the States and vice versa. The currency exchange can be intimidating, tricky—to the seller as well as the buyer."

Tugging at his briefcase, Shoe pulled out a file folder, fumbled through the papers. He looked up at Shi, his eyes piercing her eyes. "Your background, Ms. Shi, I found that you've been a U.S.

citizen for ten years. Before that, you lived in China, your native country. How did you happen to set up this real estate business here in Boston?"

"A friend of my father was a real estate broker in China. I worked for him for five years in Shanghai and then in Beijing when he opened a second office. Let's say I had an aptitude for finances. He is the one I referred to as my liaison, sharing leads. He suggested I move to America, because I spoke English and because we worked well together. He wanted to expand his business, take advantage of the opportunities that had developed, and the pent-up desire many Chinese have to invest outside of China."

"I see. Can you tell me where you were...exactly...the morning of Mr. Wu's untimely death?"

"What time would that be detective?"

"Between eight and ten o'clock," Shoe said.

"Oh, yes. I was here doing paperwork."

"Anybody with you?" Shoe asked.

"No. I was calculating my loss because of Mr. Wu, and wondering if there was any way to salvage the deal. But, I had come to the conclusion there was nothing I could do. You see, it wasn't just the sale to Mr. Wu, but the potential to sell more properties to his network of friends and family. Because of Mr. Wu's connections and the prospect of more business, I had just signed a lease for a much larger office."

"I suppose without the sale, Mr. Wu's lack of funds put you in a precarious position...financially speaking. You said you were furious?"

"Did I? Well, nothing I can't handle," Quin Shi said.

"I see. I'd like the name of your partner in Beijing, and then Ms. Bradley and I will be on our way."

"Whatever for? There is no partner, only a friendship. I see no need to alarm him. I'm the one who must cope with this mess."

"Just his name, address, and phone number, if you please, Ms. Shi."

Jeli, looked away. It was embarrassing to see her squirm. Shi's backpedalling—Shoe got under her skin. She's practically turning hostile. But I can't see her killing Mr. Wu. She's too fragile. On the other hand when money is involved, or lack of money, it can give a person great strength.

Quin glared at Shoe. Breaking eye contact, releasing a long sigh, she did what Shoe asked.

———

LEAVING QUIN SHI'S OFFICE, Detective Shoe tucked his briefcase under his arm, began strolling up the sidewalk. Jeli quickly matched his stride. "Do you still want to visit Faye Yoon with me, Ms. Bradley?" he asked.

"Yes, as Quin said, she and I only met once before, but I had several meetings with Faye Yoon. She was a big help. So I'll be interested to hear what she has to say about Mr. Wu. I met her after Josh Greely hired me. He said there was a potential buyer from China interested in the condo he was renovating."

"I see. Ms. Bradley, I have to check in at the department so I'll meet you at one o'clock, Yoon's Furniture."

The detective turned to the access ramp of the parking garage. Jeli stood a moment, a scowl forming. She'd hoped they might have lunch. She had kept quiet, listening to the back and forth with Shi and was bursting with questions. Shrugging off the annoyance, she headed for the small café a few doors from Faye's shop. She was carrying her laptop, and it would be a good time to work on a presentation, a pitch to other developers. Josh wasn't the only game in town.

Head down as before, arms tight to her parka preventing the frigid air access, she picked up her pace, eager for a hot cup of coffee. A grilled cheese sandwich would be nice to go with.

Chapter 36

———

FAYE YOON'S SHOP DOOR WAS LOCKED.

A sign hung in the window—CLOSED.

Detective Shoe and Jeli shielded their eyes from the street's reflection on the display window as they peered inside the store.

Shoe stepped back, tapped his cell.

"Hello, hello, Ms. Yoon? This is Detective Shoe. I'm at your front door...our appointment—" Frowning, he pocketed his phone, looked at Jeli. "She hung up."

Jeli pressed her nose against the window. "I see her. She's coming."

Yoon emerged from the shadows, unlocked the door. Waving them inside, she glanced at Jeli, then closed and locked the door.

"Faye, you've been crying. What's happened?" Jeli asked, her arms open as she stepped to Faye.

Faye leaned in accepting the offer of comfort, Jeli patting her back.

"I loved him...he's gone," Faye said, tears springing from under her eyelids onto Jeli's shoulder. She was dressed all in white— tunic over trousers, no jewelry.

Jeli locked eyes with Shoe, over the woman crying in her arms. A slight shake of her head, indicating she was as surprised as he at Yoon's revelation. The woman she held was fifteen, maybe twenty years Mr. Wu's junior.

Faye stepped back, fumbling for the limp hanky in her pocket, dabbed at her eyes. "I'm sorry. I didn't mean to...it's all so sudden. Come with me...to my office. We'll have tea."

Jeli gazed about as she followed behind the detective. Admiring the beautiful inventory of new and old furniture, the accessories from China, she took note of some additional pieces since her last visit.

Yoon's office was small, tidy, a sitting area in the corner with a small table in the center. Yoon pulled up her desk chair alongside the other two chairs. Tucked in the opposite corner was a drop-leaf desk. The desk was open and Jeli's eyes fixed on a picture of Faye and Mr. Wu—he in his wheelchair, she with her arms draped around him, her head pressed against his, both smiling.

"I didn't know you were coming, Jeli. I'm so happy to see you."

"Your white tunic is—"

"At the death of a friend, traditionally, white is worn by someone in mourning outside the immediate family. Those in the family wear black, or blue, for instance, but never red."

Faye wiped a fresh tear away.

"I'm sorry to intrude, Ms. Yoon," Detective Shoe said. "The picture on your desk—you had a personal relationship with Mr. Wu?"

"You're not intruding, Detective. Frankly, it's a relief to speak openly about him. Wu Chao and I have been in love for many years…after his wife died. Our families did not approve. It was very hard on us, so we decided if I moved away, to America, then perhaps he could visit, we could see each other, spend time with each other away from disapproving eyes."

"Excuse me, Ms. Yoon. Wu Chao—his full name?" Shoe said.

"Yes, but in China the family name is said before the given name."

"Faye, you said, when Susan Li first introduced us, that you had contacts in China, as well as around the States and—" Jeli began.

"That's right. You see, the one-child-rule in China kept families small, so families band together, and friends of each family become a network. My family had a network, predominately in business—furniture shops. So when I suggested opening a shop in Boston they were all for it. They didn't know my real reason—to spend time alone with Wu Chao whenever he could travel to be with me. His grandson, being an American citizen, made it fairly easy for Wu Chao to renew his passport and visa with a family member sponsorship."

"I'm sorry, Ms. Yoon, but I must ask where you were the morning of Mr. Wu's death, between the hours of eight and ten o'clock."

"I was here, in the shop until I left to go to the condo where I saw you, Detective, and you took my name."

"Did you have...well, did Mr. Wu pay you for the furniture?" Shoe asked.

"At first, Jeli asked if I could loan her the furniture to stage the property for a potential client. Hopefully, it would result in a sale, she said, adding there was no guarantee. I agreed. Any shop would jump at the chance. At the time I didn't know the connection with the condo, Wu Chao, and Ms. Bradley. I didn't know until Wu Chao called, telling me how delighted he was with everything, and surprised that Ms. Bradley had circumvented Mr. Alex Chen. Wu Chao and I didn't think it wise for me to be involved with his move to Boston. We were afraid the families would learn the move would be permanent. We were going to continue to keep our love a secret, so he arranged with my competitor, Mr. Chen, that he would be looking to him to furnish his Boston property."

"But Mr. Chen must have found out that he was not in the deal for furniture?" Shoe asked.

"Oh, yes he did. Mr. Chen stormed into my shop. He was furious to lose the deal, because as I've said, it wasn't just Wu Chao's extended family, but also those in his network would be following. Mr. Chen knows of the loyalty of a Chinese network and so he was out of a substantial amount of business." Faye shook her head. "I remember that day. Mr. Chen was so mad I thought he might have a heart attack right here in my shop. He said he was going to kill Wu Chao for—" Ms. Yoon stopped midsentence, her hand covering her mouth. "Oh, I didn't mean to imply...Mr. Chen may have been mad at losing the business, but he would never have...you know, harmed Wu Chao. Oh, no, no."

Horrified at what she had divulged, Yoon was overcome by another round of tears.

"Ms. Yoon, I'm so sorry...Ms. Bradley and I will be going. If I have any more questions, I'll give you a call. I'm sorry for your loss."

Jeli hugged Faye, whispering in her ear, "Susan and I will stop in soon. If you want to talk...you know, woman to woman, call me anytime."

Detective Shoe waited at the front door, then he and Jeli walked out of Faye Yoon's *New and Antique Furniture and Accessories from China*.

Ambling down the sidewalk to the corner where they would part, Shoe stopped in the middle of the sidewalk looking off down the street. "Ms. Bradley, you never know what you're going to find on a person's private life when you start peeling back the onion."

"That's for sure, Detective."

"No matter what Ms. Yoon said, she certainly threw her competitor, Mr. Chen, under the bus. How much would you bet that Chen will counter that he never said he'd kill Mr. Wu?"

"I'll take you up on that bet and raise you one." Jeli said laughing. "Call me anytime, Detective, if you have more questions."

"And you, Ms. Bradley, call me if another piece of information trips the neurons in that bouncing brain of yours."

Chapter 37

——

THE SUN SET, DUSK turned to night. Jeli stared at her reflection in the train's window. Every now and then the lights of a small town interchanged with her reflection.

Jeli had packed a small case, wrote a quick note for Susan that she was going to the farm for a couple of days. She propped the note up on Mr. Coffee, and left for the T-station. While waiting to board she made two quick calls. One to Georgie asking if he could pick her up at the Portsmouth station and could he let Mom and Pop know she was coming home. He said yes to both.

As the train sped by a cluster of houses, she imagined families eating dinner around a table, people swapping stories about their day. So many thoughts entered her mind, one quickly replacing another. She was tired. The events of the past few days left more questions than answers—both personally, and larger ramifications for those around her.

She was still stunned learning of Faye's revelation, her despair over losing the love of her life due to Wu's murder. A love held secret for so many years only to have an end she was not prepared for, an end to her dreams of at last being with him. Faye must have an enormous heart, Jeli thought. Wanting to care for him...maybe Billy Qiáng would have stayed on. Billy, what was he going to do? What did he say...go back to Beijing, or was it to stay in Boston? She couldn't remember. She did remember mentioning Billy to Marshall.

Her head hurt.

Georgie gave her a hug as she bumped off the train with her case and a heavy tote over her shoulder. Sliding into the car, she immediately fell into a comfortable silence, head back, eyes closed. Georgie drove through the darkness, sensing she wasn't ready to talk. That would come after dinner, maybe over a nightcap of brandy in front of a roaring fire in the fireplace and the comfort of the farmhouse, the comfort of being home.

Mom and Pops and Gran pulled her into warm embraces, as she entered the house. She looked tired in her parka, red curls restricted in a ponytail held back by an elastic band. Pops suggested she take a warm bath, and then come down to dinner whenever she was ready—cut-up chicken, sweet potatoes, onion, and rosemary in three large slow cookers.

Jeli thanked them, said she'd be ready for dinner in a half hour—a hot bath was very appealing.

Her family exchanged glances hearing Jeli bump up the two flights of stairs to her room. Where was their vibrant, full-of-fun-Anjelica?

Jeli didn't linger, she took a quick shower instead of a long bath. No point letting herself sink into a funk, she was looking for support from her family, telling them what had transpired, get their thoughts on how she was going to conquer the bats fighting in her head over how to move forward.

Forward!

Suddenly she was hungry. Pulling on a pair of warm fleecy sweatpants and a top, she smiled as she slipped the pink fluffy kittens on her feet. The kittens hustled down the steps to the kitchen with the fire blazing from fresh logs. The tantalizing smell of chicken with rosemary tickled her nose as she kissed Gran setting out the dinner plates.

Wolfe and Georgie entered the kitchen boosted on a blast of frigid air. Georgie slapped his gloves together, stuffing them into the pockets of his parka. "I talked to Finn and Cameron. They're finishing up some work down at the barn. Said to go ahead, they'll be along later with the rest of their families."

Pops looked up and smiled as Jeli slid onto the chair beside him. She looked more like her sparkly self. "That's my girl. Nothing is going to keep you down. Some chicken?"

"Yes, please, that big piece of thigh and a leg. So, everyone, you'll never guess what I've been up to the past few weeks. Go ahead, give it a try. I dare you."

"Just tell us, dear," Gran said. "You're certainly bursting with energy. Thirty minutes ago you looked like you'd lost your best friend."

"Didn't lose a friend, Gran. I have a new BFF. Her name is Susan Li. She works for Marshall. She's very smart...a programmer writing all kinds of code that I have no clue about. She asked me to share her apartment and I immediately accepted. I didn't want to cramp my oldest brother's style."

"Certainly, Marshall didn't ask you to leave did—"

"No, Mom. But he only has one bedroom. I didn't dare leave my things out...you know how he and Sadie are—neat freaks."

"Help yourself to the sweet potatoes, Jeli," Pops said. "You must invite Susan to the farm some weekend...soon. So we can meet her."

"Definitely on my bucket list."

"Anjelica. A bucket list at your age?" Gran scoffed with a twinkle in her eye.

"Susan and I are like sisters. I feel totally comfortable with her. And then, only today, I learned of a twenty-year-old love affair between a man and a woman. A Chinese woman Susan introduced me to who owns a furniture store. An affair she kept secret until this very day. And then there are the two men who are after me—I haven't decided if I want to be caught, and if I do, which one do I let catch me? And then...there's this murder topping it all off."

"Murder?" Pops said, setting his fork down on his plate.

Pleased that she had everyone's attention, Jeli took a sip of rosé wine.

"I'm okay with your sharing an apartment with your new friend Susan." Jane started the plate of chicken pieces around the table. "Let's start with the two men...trying to catch you. Work up to the murder."

"Well, they are different, very different. One is very polite, considerate, and the other is brash, can be very irritating, and is totally hot."

"Hot?" Gran said. "Really, Anjelica Jane, I never."

"Wait, Gran. The second one is my boss, or was until the client died. Make that, the one who was murdered."

"Are you in danger?" Wolfe asked. "Can't be a good situation."

"Travis said I should be careful."

Everyone looked at her.

"Oh, it's okay. He saw my name on a list of people who are being interviewed—you know, where you were between eight and ten in the morning," Jeli said, mocking Detective Shoe's voice. "Oh, and one more piece of information, I found the body." she said grinning.

"Anjelica, murder is not funny," Gran said.

"Sorry, no it's not. The murdered man is Chinese. There are some unusual circumstances surrounding the murder, and that's why the report was transmitted from Boston to Washington. All very complicated. You'd have to ask Travis how that works."

"Are you being careful? You've never lived in a big city," Pops said.

"Marshall gave me some tips—always check for an escape route in a restaurant before choosing a table, always choose a table in the middle to the back of the restaurant. Sadly these days, like all the turmoil in Paris, you shouldn't pick a seat because it's your favorite. Safety first."

Jane locked eyes with her husband. What was their daughter getting into?

Jeli continued, as much as she was enjoying the surprises she had just divulged, she also didn't want to alarm them. None of it was funny, as Gran had said.

"The two men I thought I might be falling in love with are Josh Greely, my boss—who may not be for long because his client is dead, and Charles Wurthy—grandson of the murdered man. But with everything going on the past few days, I don't trust my judgment. But, the big positive development, I feel I'm finally on the right path—interior design. The architecture part is very useful in understanding the bones of a space." Jeli stabbed a piece of sweet potato, chewing thoughtfully.

"I've learned so much, especially with Susan's help. She's Chinese. Went to MIT, and after several years she took the oath of citizenship. Anyway, through her introducing me to the Chinese furniture owner, I've learned a lot about the Chinese culture...meeting new people, clients...something new at every corner...I think I'll keep going down this road. So be happy that the baby of the family may be on her way in the world, and, rest assured, she's not going to make any snap moves."

"Let's all drink to that," Georgie said raising his glass. "Here's to the baby of the family...all grown up."

Jeli nodded to each in turn then took a sip of wine, the pink kittens bouncing on the wide pine floorboards in the 1840 farmhouse.

The next morning, after blueberry pancakes with a side of scrambled eggs, Georgie jumped in his car, turned the key in the ignition, as Jeli waved goodbye to the family. Pops put his arms around his wife on one side and his mother on the other. "Our baby is definitely grown up, grown up with grown up problems and adventures."

———

"GEORGIE, STOP THE CAR. Finn's coming out of the barn."

Jeli popped out of the car, ran into Finn's arms. He twirled her around, the pair laughing, then he set her on her feet.

"Sorry I missed you at dinner last night, Jeli-bean. Georgie filled me in after you went to bed. Murder? Should I worry about you?"

"Not yet. I'll call if I need a hit man. How are you? Looks like married life suits you."

"It has to be the right person, and Katie is definitely the right one, the only one. And little Daisy...God, Jeli, I swear she's going on seventeen, but she barely comes up to my chest."

"Sounds wonderful. And the brewpub? Opening still scheduled for late March?"

"Yup, but it may slip to April. No matter when, promise me you'll be here. I'll need your spirit."

"Wouldn't miss it. Have to run. So much to catch up on. Next time, Finn, you and me, a talk over your best brew. Deal?"

"Deal."

Jeli gave her brother a fierce hug, then jumped back into the car.

"He looks happy," Jeli said to Georgie as she fastened her seatbelt.

"He is. He had a rough patch after the divorce but he turned it all around when Katie and Daisy became part of his life."

"How about you, Georgie? Is there a lady in your life?"

"No time, Jeli. With the hops and barley crops, I'm out flat. Seems like I plant, it rains, I harvest—two or more plantings a year. I'm finishing up my research, took a class at the University of New Hampshire over the freezing months, and I'm raring to go for the planting season."

"Finn is so lucky to have you. Hey, any Rosemary sightings?"

"None since you and I were in the attic. How's the dresser set? Any vibes?"

Jeli laughed. "I hold up the hand mirror every morning—

Mirror, mirror in my hand,

tell me, tell me my life's plan."

"And the answer is?"

"No word yet, but I keep trying. We're here...just drop me off. Thanks for the lift. Love ya."

Jeli threw Georgie a kiss.

Invigorated from her visit to the farm, Jeli strutted off to catch the train to Boston, her mind wandering to the big question—who killed Mr. Wu?

Chapter 38

———

THE CLICKITY-CLACK OF the train speeding south over the tracks, her body listing right, then left as the train rounded a curve, only heightened Jeli's eagerness to return to Boston. Some passengers slept to the rocking of the train but not Jeli, not today. She had received a call from Josh just as she boarded, asking her to dinner with his family tonight. Mr. Greely Senior was anxious to meet her.

So, maybe she had a job after all. In any event she had formulated a plan, a plan as yet that had not been revealed to anyone. After Josh's call, she texted Susan that she was having dinner with him, but she needed some serious girl talk tonight. Susan texted her back from work that she was up for a gabfest and would pick up a new supply of marshmallows.

———

NOT HIS USUAL PATTERN, Josh picked her up in a shiny black sedan. She wondered if it was his father's car, and also wondered if the senior Greely told his son he should fetch Ms. Bradley.

"Nice car, Josh. Yours? Your father's?"

"The old man's. He said if I asked a lady home to dinner, I should pick her up."

Jeli looked out the window, a slight grin playing with her lips. She had guessed right. "I believe you said your father's a developer. Does he want you to join his business?"

"Not a good subject, Red. Steer clear of his business dealings."

"Sure. Does your mother work?"

"You could say that—works at being the president of any charity that has an opening."

Jeli turned in her seat, against the seatbelt. "You're either in a cranky mood or you don't want me to come to dinner. I don't have to...come to dinner. I can play the 'I've-come-down-with-the-flu' card."

"I'm sorry, Red. Definitely a bad mood, but my parents asked to meet you, and I'd like you to meet them. I want you to understand why I have to make a go of my own business, which now has been short-circuited with Wu's death."

Josh smacked the steering wheel. "I poured everything into that building. Not only did the deal fall through with Wu's bounced check, but then he dies. His dying leaves me no chance to restructure the sale. It probably wouldn't work anyway." Josh sighed as he turned into a circular drive in front of a very large colonial house—red brick, white shutters, extensions on either side, and white columns defining a portico. Jeli wasn't ready for a stately mansion. She was suddenly glad she had chosen a little black dress instead of jeweled jeans.

"Sit tight. I'll get your door. Mother's probably peeking out the window."

Josh walked around and opened her door.

Another first.

Walking up the three steps banked with lush evergreens on either side, he paused before opening the door. "We can leave whenever we want," he said.

Jeli didn't reply. *Actually, how bad can it be?* she thought.

Josh stepped up to the door at the same time a good looking older gentleman with salt and pepper hair opened the door. He was wearing a light tan jacket, leather patches at the elbows, over a white turtleneck sweater. Josh was the spitting image of his father without the smile that is. It was only then that she remembered seeing him at the condo during the chaos of finding Wu's body.

"Ms. Bradley, I assume," he said smiling. "Nice to meet you, properly this time. I'm Mr. Greely," salt-and-pepper man said, extending his hand, pumping hers. "Come in, come in. This is my wife, Mrs. Greely."

Jeli smiled sweetly, thought better of extending her hand to Mrs. Greely, who stood with her hands clasped behind her back.

"I thought we'd have cocktails in the library before dinner," she said turning away. "Joshua, help Ms. Bradley with her coat, then come along."

Josh rolled his eyes at Jeli—I told you so—as he helped her out of her coat, hung it in the hall closet, and then followed his parents, escorting her to the library.

In contrast to the odd introduction to Mrs. Greely at the door, the library was cozy, inviting—two settees facing each other across a mahogany antique coffee table with pie-crust edges. A gentle fire flickered in the green-marble fireplace.

"I mixed a pitcher of Manhattans—okay with everyone?" Mr. Greely asked stepping to a small wet bar tucked in the corner of the room.

With no response, Mr. Greely served the drinks and then settled on a wingback chair to the left of the fireplace between the hearth and the settees. Mrs. Greely sat in a matching chair on the other side. Both looked at her—Mr. Greely with a friendly smile, Mrs. Greely with a steely stare.

"Ms. Bradley, when I stopped at the condo, the morning Josh's client died, I did take a quick look around. The staging was spectacular, so appropriate to entice a buyer from China. Were you responsible for the design with—"

"All mine, Mr. Greely. When Josh told me his client was from China I was lucky to have a friend from Beijing, and she introduced me to a furniture dealer, Faye Yoon. I learned everything I know, which of course is still limited, from the two of them—my friend and Ms. Yoon. So, I'd say, the staging was all mine, but learning what would be appropriate came from them. I picked from their suggestions."

"Joshua, you were smart to hire such a talented designer," Mr. Greely said.

Mrs. Greely looked up at the door, nodded. "Sybille's ready to serve." She stood, leaving her empty glass on the lamp table beside her chair.

Jeli took her clue from Mr. Greely, who followed his wife but carried the balance of his cocktail with him.

Dinner passed along, during which Mrs. Greely had another cocktail and two glasses of wine. She launched into her arduous efforts keeping numerous charities and clubs afloat. Between the beef wellington and dessert, Josh and his father excused themselves for a private conversation out in the hall. Mrs. Greely didn't miss a beat relating, in her soft-spoken voice, yet another story of the lackluster women she had to deal with.

Jeli only half listened, giving a nod or a shake of her head to Mrs. Greely's current lament. Her attention was on the voices in the hall that kept rising. She didn't catch the first few minutes of the conversation, but then father and son began shouting at each other.

"He's dead, father. No sale."

"What are you going to do? Don't think you can come crawling back to me for help. If you don't want any part of my business, then you're on your own. Chinese are superstitious. The man dying in the condo will be considered a bad omen. You'd better sell it quick as you can to another Chinese to change the superstition from bad chi to good chi."

"I don't need your help, father, and I didn't ask to come to dinner."

Josh stormed into the dining room. "Come on, Red. Dinner is over. We'll stop for coffee on the way back to your place. Don't worry, father, I'll take my own car." Josh fished in his pants pocket, withdrawing a set of car keys. He threw them down on the table causing his mother to jump at the interruption in her dialogue.

Jeli thanked Mrs. Greely for dinner, nodded to Mr. Greely and followed Josh. He grabbed her coat out of the hall closet, brusquely helped her into it, grasped her elbow and marched her out the door.

"Wait here. I'll get my car," he called over his shoulder.

Jeli texted Susan that she was going to be late, too late for girl talk. *Tomorrow night?*

Chapter 39

———

THE AROMA OF FRESH brewed coffee slid under the door of Jeli's bedroom. Rolling onto her back, she stared at the ceiling. The sharp voices of Josh and his father the night before twisted around his mother's never-ending complaints about the people in her social circle.

A soft knock on her door shoved the Greely family from her thoughts. "Come on in, Susan. I'm on a permanent-vacation day."

Susan opened the door, a cup of coffee in one hand, gloves ready to be pulled on in the other. "Brought you some coffee. It's piping hot. You were in late last night. I have to skedaddle—Marshall's staff meeting this morning. Are we on for tonight—a gabfest?"

"Absolutely. And don't do any shopping on your way home. I'll check the fridge and run out to add what's missing."

"Sounds good. Pick up a bottle of wine to go with. See you tonight. I'll call if I get held up."

Jeli fluffed up the pillow against the headboard, pulling the patterned quilt of red, white, and blue pieces of cotton fabric under her chin. She left just enough room to sip her coffee, being careful not to spill. Glancing at the clock, she was surprised to see it was close to nine. Normally a light sleeper, she was an up-and-at 'em girl in the early morning with the call of the farm's rooster.

Her mind again drifted back to last night. Mrs. Greely was a nut case or an alcoholic, probably both. But she rather liked Mr. Greely, other than his attitude toward his son. But who was she to say that Josh didn't deserve a kick in the butt. There was an obvious conflict between the two. Maybe it was a competition thing. She'd read about that in some families.

Her thoughts returned to Susan and the gabfest. She'd made notes on the plan she was going to present to Susan. The plan on how to go forward, the next step in her so-called career, Jeli wanted her friend's input, ideas. Her notes still needed tweaking. The coffee shop down the street would be a good place to hangout for a few hours—better with some hustle bustle of people—more stimulating than the stillness of the apartment.

She showered, dressed in warm corduroy slacks, a heavy sweater with swirls of bright colors and ankle boots. Standing in front of the dresser mirror, she pulled a knit cap over her springy red curls just as the Saints began to march. Smiling at the caller ID, she put the cell to her ear.

"Hey, Charlie, what's up?"

"Nothing really. Can we meet for lunch…say at eleven?"

"That's doable. Where?"

"Wherever. You name it."

"I was just going out to a cafe—working on a game plan for my life's journey. I'll text you the name, the street. You can Google it. Are you okay? You sound dumpy."

"Dumpy. That about sums it up. See ya."

―――

THE CAFÉ PROVED PERFECT, just enough bustle, but not so much to be distracting. Checking her watch, noting it was close to eleven, she put her laptop in her tote along with a pad of paper, preparing to wait for Charlie. She saw him entering, looked around, caught her wave. *Oh, oh,* she thought. *Droopy and dumpy. Not a good sign.*

He paused, asked the waitress for a cup of coffee and joined Jeli at the corner booth.

"Thanks for meeting me, Anjelica. Finish your life's plan?"

"Pretty much. How's work going for you? It's a little early—"

"I didn't go to work. Played hooky the last few days. Nothing seems to matter anymore."

The waitress set down his coffee, asked if they wanted to order. Both shook their heads.

Jeli reached across the table, laying her hand over his. "Charlie, you're grieving over your grandfather's sudden death. Give yourself some time—"

"Time? That's all I have. My father is holed up in his office and…Anjelica, my family is gone…everyone—mother, grandfather. My father may as well be dead for all that I see him. He doesn't care…maybe never did. I've always been an annoyance."

His words were startling. She couldn't fathom being an annoyance to her family. Challenging maybe, but annoyance? She looked away not able to respond. Better to change the subject.

"Charlie, have you ever heard of Faye Yoon? Did your grandfather ever mention her?"

"He leaned back against the booth, hands clasped over his head, his pain-filled eyes on her. "No. Who's she?"

"Umm, let me tell you a story—a true life story. Detective Shoe invited me, actually I asked if I could come along, to take Ms. Yoon's statement. You probably don't remember, or I never said, Faye is the Chinese shopkeeper who helped me stage the furniture when your grandfather first looked at the condo."

Jeli searched Charlie's face for any sign of recognition. His eyes were blank, shifting away. Jeli patted his hand to bring his attention back to what she was telling him.

"Charlie, she had a picture in her office. It was of your grandfather in his wheelchair. Faye Yoon was standing behind him, bent forward, her cheek to his, arms draped around his shoulders."

Jeli patted his hand again—this was important.

"Charlie, when the detective and I arrived, Faye's eyes were red, swollen from crying. She told us that she and your grandfather had been in love for years."

"In love? Surely not lovers, he was—"

"Romantic love…maybe not sexual—"

"When?"

"Since after your mother died. They kept it a secret because the family, you, his network of friends, would be against it. Awhile ago they hatched a plan. She would come to America, Boston, to establish a furniture shop with the help of her family. Once established, your grandfather planned to join her...here. His buying the condo was a first step, but I guess he lost most of his money in the downturn of the stock market."

"Wait, there was a woman. She would visit when I was staying for the summer with my grandfather in Beijing. But, as I recall, they seemed to be engaged in business discussions. She never stayed long—cup of tea maybe—I wonder if Faye Yoon is that woman. Probably not. He would have told me if there was someone so important..."

Jeli rooted around her tote, retrieving Faye's business card. She pressed it into Charlie's hand.

"Go see her, Charlie. You'll like her. I think you two can help each other—you're both suffering a great loss of the same person, the loss of a man you both loved."

Chapter 40

———

CANDLES, A BOTTLE OF CHIANTI, and the aroma of baking bread permeated the small apartment. The cutting board was set with Swiss cheese, corn beef—the must have ingredients for Reuben sandwiches, along with a jar of spicy mustard, a jar of sauerkraut and Russian dressing. The gabfest setting greeted Susan as she walked in the door.

Stopping in her tracks, she glanced from the candles on the coffee table, to the kitchen counter, to Jeli—pink kittens peeking from under black sweats.

"Is this a gabfest or a séance?" Susan said, grinning.

"Take your pick. I ran out of time so I raided the deli counter down the street. Hungry?" Jeli asked, uncorking the wine, pouring a sample into each goblet.

"Starving. I don't remember these glasses—"

"We have to have the proper ambience when discussing our life's journey into the future. Yes, I said *our journey* just in case you're deliberating on your future, too. Now, change into something comfy. The bread is ready to come out of the oven, and then we can build our Reubens anyway we like—with or without sauerkraut."

Jeli slipped on the oven mitt setting the hot bread on top of the stove. "How was the staff meeting?" she called out, removing the golden loaf from the pan.

"Marshall has big plans for the company," Susan said as she joined Jeli. "There, now I'm ready to dive into this divine spread."

"Wait, wait," Jeli said handing a goblet to Susan. "Here's to us and our futures. Futures to be defined tonight."

The girls clinked the rims of their goblets in the candlelight, then set about building their sandwiches.

Curled up on opposite ends of the couch, they took a bite with a sip of wine.

"Where are you going to start? Please don't say when you were born," Susan said, wiping a dab of mustard off her chin before it dropped to her green flannel PJs.

"Nope. This epiphany came to me a couple of days ago. I got to thinking about Josh and Charlie. Josh—egotistical, exciting, hot. Charlie—gentleman, thoughtful, a bit boring. I have experienced some rather sensuous kisses from both."

"Hey, have you been holding out on me? Did you do the...you know...the wild thing—sex?"

"No, but I wasn't prepared for the feeling that I wanted to...the wild thing. I was falling for two men, polar opposites."

"Jeli, you barely know them. As you said, Josh is hot—your hormones were flaring. Charlie, well, your feelings for him could be mixed up with sympathy for the loss of his grandfather."

"There's definitely something about the sympathy thing." Jeli retrieved the bottle, poured more deep red wine, while relating her visit with Faye Yoon.

"Do you think Charlie will go see her," Susan asked.

"I do. Anyway, in trying to sort out my feelings, I came to the realization that I wasn't ready for a serious relationship with anyone. Susan, meeting you, our conversations with Faye Yoon, the incredible rush when Mr. Wu saw the condo for the first time...everything I designed for him...he got it. If that's the rush you get when you love what you're doing, when my creative side kicks in...well, that's what I want. I don't want to settle. I don't ever want to stop reaching for the next rush."

"You definitely have boatloads of talent...no, you have a passion for design. And I know what you mean by a rush—when I'm coding a software program and the string of commands begin to flow, and the results are even better than I expected, and then Marshall wants to see more, giving me ideas of where I can take the program, whew. It's heady stuff."

Jeli cocked her head, playing over what Susan said and the way she said it. "Susan, do you have a crush on Marshall?"

A flush crept up Susan's face. "Oh, no...maybe a little...but he doesn't see me as anything but a programmer. Don't you dare say a word of this to him. Promise me you won't. I'd have to leave the company. Promise?"

"I promise." Jeli pulled a zipper over her lips. "Back to Josh and Charlie—fun dates but no more than dates, at least not right away. Susan, I want to build my design business. First, I'll concentrate on decorating around the Chinese culture. Between you and Faye, I found it fascinating and I've only skimmed the surface. I want to travel to China, but no way could I pick up the language. Could you come with me? Maybe stay a week, a month—between your programming projects? Sometime? Do you think you could?"

"I think so. I may have a break in May or June. That would be a nice time of year. In May, Beijing's filled with bright reds and vivid greens, flowers everywhere. Normally, the temperature is between fifty to seventy degrees, warm, even hot. There may be some drizzle but clear and sunny days are in the majority. You'd love it. You could meet my family, and my father would love to introduce you to his business friends. Who knows where that could lead."

"Quin said she has clients lined up who want to buy property. Of course, that would mean I would work exclusively for Josh, at least for awhile...that may be a problem when I branch out on my own," Jeli said, pouring the remaining drops of wine.

"Listen to you...branching out already."

"Susan, we could travel other places together—Greece perhaps. Places where people are worried about their money and want to invest in property in the States."

Mulling over the future Jeli outlined, they fell into a comfortable silence. A classical playlist set to repeat on her computer, softly caressed their imagination—Beethoven, Rachmaninoff—wondering if the thoughts they exchanged could possibly pan out, even if just a little. Jeli's plans were more than exciting, they were filled with challenges, thrilling to contemplate.

"Planning our future is exhausting. Let's put the food stuff away and go to bed," Jeli said, sipping the last of her wine.

"That was the most delicious, stimulating gabfest I've ever had," Susan said with a giggle.

"Oh, I forgot to tell you," Jeli said, walking to the kitchen sink. "Charlie called just before you got home. He invited me to dinner with his father tomorrow night, which should be interesting. First, Josh's father and now Charlie's."

"Sounds to me, when a boy brings a girl to meet papa, the boy has something serious in mind."

"Doesn't matter. No relationships for me—but dates are fun. Night. Don't forget about our trip to China," Jeli said over her shoulder.

"I'm in. It's time for me to recharge with my own family...like you at the farm."

Chapter 41

———

EMERALDS SPARKLED IN JELI'S eyes as they popped open, a smile slowly growing to a wide grin. Today was day one of her future. Adrenalin pumped through her veins as she freed her legs from the patchwork quilt. Sitting on the edge of the bed, her eyes roamed about the room.

"What to do first?"

"That was easy." The Saints insisted she answer her cell.

"Hi, Charlie. How are you today?"

"Can I ask you a favor?"

"Sure. Are you at work?" Jeli asked.

"No. But after seeing you...well, I'd like to meet Faye Yoon. Can you go with me this afternoon? Help break the ice?"

Jeli smiled at herself in the mirror hanging on the closet door. How perfect is this? Step one, make an arrangement with Faye for future design work using her inventory. It's like a fortuneteller showing the way. Wait til Susan hears.

"I'd love to go with you. There's a bookstore, The Story Teller, two shops down. I'll meet you there. How about two o'clock?"

"Thanks, Anjelica. This doesn't cancel dinner with my dad tonight. Okay?"

"Okey-dokey. See you at two."

Setting her phone down, Jeli wondered if she should call Faye or just walk in with Charlie. Looking in the mirror as she brushed her hair with Rosemary's dresser set, she imagined what Rosemary would say. "Not a problem, Ms. Bradley. Call her. Say you'd like to drop by at two if she'll be there. That'll do it. Besides, it's all true—business and pleasure. Your business—Charlie's pleasure...hopefully."

Shuffling to the kitchen, she pushed Mr. Coffee's button Susan had set up before leaving for work. A fresh pot of coffee, and a microwave serving of oatmeal, Gran would be proud.

"Okay, Ms. Bradley, what's step two? Umm, of course, your website, silly. Make it sparkle."

———

IF THE MOON WAS aligned with Capricorn, her astrological sign, the day couldn't have been better. Waiting for Charlie at The Story Teller, Jeli asked the clerk where she might find a book on designing a website for a small business. The girl walked to the graphics section, checked the spines, then pulled two books from the shelf for Jeli to look at. She also suggested checking out the business section.

One was right-on. She stepped to the cashier at the same time Charlie walked in the door. Turning to him, he grasped her hand, pulling her into a hug, whispering how much he appreciated her going with him to meet Faye Yoon.

The whisper tickled her ear, causing a slight lurch in her stomach—*maybe he's not so boring.*

Stashing the new web-design book in her tote, her hand in his, they left the bookstore and moments later entered Faye Yoon's shop.

Jeli didn't know how Faye was going to react when she saw Charlie, which is why she didn't tell her he wanted to meet her, and yes, she hoped Faye wouldn't be upset that she had revealed her secret to Charlie.

Hearing the chime on the shop door, Faye stepped out of her office. Seeing Charlie, her jaw dropped, her hand gripping a nearby chair back for support.

Charlie scrunched his brows, forehead furrowed, trying to place the woman dressed in white standing a few yards from him.

"Faye?" he said, his voice barely a whisper.

Faye stared at him, then slowly nodded. She turned back to her office, softly asking him to follow.

Charlie looked at Jeli, questioning eyes, he grasped her hand, giving a slight tug to come with him.

They stood in the small office filled with treasures Faye had collected over the years, mementos one picks up through life's journey. Some worth more than a thousand dollars, some pocket change, altogether priceless. Faye picked up the picture in the back of her secretary, handed it to Charlie. It was the picture of her with his grandfather, happier days, a secret rendezvous.

He stared at the couple in the picture, then handed the gold-leaf frame back to Faye. "Why didn't Grandfather tell me about you? So many times I felt guilty at the end of a vacation, guilty for leaving him alone."

"My family, his network of friends, didn't approve. The age difference for one, the other...my family had picked out someone else for me. When I refused they thought me foolish, although they wholeheartedly approved of my move to America, and of my starting a business. Of course, the business helped them as well. So Wu Chao and I felt it easier on everyone to keep our feelings to ourselves. He loved you, Charlie. You were the light of his life. Moving to Boston—he felt he would have the best of both worlds —you and me. We were going to tell you once he was settled." A tear rolled down her porcelain cheek. Wiping it away with the back of her hand, she set the picture of her lover on top of the desk, a slight smile crossing her lips. At last her love for him was out in the open.

"My father? Does he know?" Charlie said.

"Oh my, no. I didn't know your grandfather when you were born, before your mother died. After we met, he spoke of you all the time, absolutely giddy when he knew you were coming for summer vacation. Each time you left to travel back to the States, he delighted in telling me over and over what you said, what the two of you did, and then how smart you were with the computer, especially the software programs you wrote. So proud you maintained your easy way, proficiency with the Chinese language."

Charlie slumped onto the delicate side chair, head bent, elbows on his thighs, hands rubbing his forehead.

"I miss him, Faye."

"I know you do, and so do I."

"I can barely put one step in front of the other," Charlie said, his voice soft, melancholy.

"He's left a deep hole in both our hearts, Charlie. Don't try to forget him. He meant too much to us. Instead, think of him. Let your heart speak to him. He will answer. He will guide you. Share your hopes and dreams and—"

"I have no more dreams, no hope...all died with him."

Faye knelt in front of Charlie, grasped his hand, holding it to her cheek. "Charlie, your dreams will return, keep putting one step in front of the other, everyday, one more step."

"Faye, do you want me to tell Dad—"

"No, no, Charlie. There was ill will between your father and your grandfather. Always, from the first time I met your grandfather. He would never explain why, always changed the subject."

Charlie shook his head. He didn't understand.

Faye stood, smiled at Jeli. "Thank you for bringing Charlie to me," she whispered.

Charlie slowly got to his feet. "Faye, can we have dinner sometime...soon?"

"I'd like that."

Charlie wrapped the delicate Chinese woman in a warm embrace, holding her to him. Breaking away, he said goodbye, promising he'd call in a few days.

Faye looked at Jeli. "I think there was something you wanted to talk about, or was that just a ruse to be sure I was in the shop?"

"Both, but I'll come back tomorrow, if that's okay?"

"I look forward to it."

Out on the sidewalk, Charlie inhaled a deep breath of the cool fresh air. "Dinner with my dad tonight?"

"You bet."

"I'll pick you up. Seven-thirty?"

"Seven-thirty."

Charlie wrapped her in his arms as he had Faye minutes earlier, but unlike with Faye, he lifted Jeli's chin touching his lips to her, the kiss becoming warmer. With a sigh, he looked into her eyes, then turned and walked down the street.

Ba-da-bing!

Chapter 42

———

A STORM WAS BREWING.

Clouds, black as the night, covered the stars, leaving one only to imagine the moonlight. At seven-thirty sharp, Charlie pressed the buzzer mounted on the brick entrance to the apartment building. The speaker crackled with Jeli's voice telling him to hang on a minute, she'd be right down.

Emerging minutes later, she glanced at the sky, then with a smile accepted his peck on her cheek.

The sidewalk was dry but Charlie held her arm, just in case she stepped on a patch of ice in her high heels. They chit-chatted in the car—the weather in general, the pending snowstorm specifically, no idea what his father planned for dinner—steering clear, for the moment, of the meeting with Faye Yoon earlier, and the kiss. Fifteen minutes later he turned the car onto a tree-lined street, lights filtering through the bones of the mighty maples, their brilliant leaves of last summer rotting under the snow cover.

Another turn, Charlie let up on the gas, coasting up the driveway of a modest cape-style house, the clapboard siding a weathered gray. The walkway to the front door was icy. Shoveling had been haphazard at best. Jeli picked her way, holding tight to Charlie's arm.

Charlie opened the front door, calling out as they stepped inside, quickly closing the door against a gust of frigid air.

"Dad, we're here."

"I'm in the living room...throwing another log on the fire."

Charlie helped Jeli out of her car coat, laying both coats on a chair next to the vestibule table. He led the way to the living room which was warm and cozy, as opposed to the chill of the slate entrance hall. The blaze of the fire and two table lamps provided an inviting glow to the overstuffed sofa, a lounger on one side facing a wingback chair on the other side.

Stan Wurthy stood by the fireplace warming his hands. He smiled at Jeli. "Nice to see you, Ms. Bradley, under better circumstance than when I first saw you...at Mr. Wu's condo."

"Nice to see you, too. Looks like we're in for a nasty night."

"Oh? How so?"

"The storm...snow, more than a foot by morning."

"Oh. Yes...the storm."

"So, Charlie, this is your childhood home?" Jeli said. "Cozy. I love a Cape Cod house."

"Charles spent his summers, school holidays in China. With boarding school, he wasn't here that much, but I guess you could call it a childhood home. Charlie, how about fixing Ms. Bradley a cocktail, or a glass of wine?"

"Wine would be lovely, thanks." Jeli's eyes roamed about the room—tidy, but lacking a woman's touch. Then she remembered Charlie saying his mother had died in a car accident, that he never really knew her. Jeli surmised that Mr. Wurthy never remarried. She made a mental note to ask Charlie about that later.

Jeli tried to make conversation, but every new topic quickly reached a dead end. Pouring a second glass of wine, Charlie turned to his father, lifting a bottle of whiskey, nodded his head, asking if he would like more. Stan held out his glass.

"Dad, have you ever heard of a Ms. Yoon...a friend of Grandfather's?"

Stan had moved from the wingback chair to the lounger, stood again, changing chairs, poking at the fire as he did so.

"No, not that I remember. Should I?"

"Anjelica took me to this woman's shop today...she's...she said she moved here from Beijing. Anjelica chose furniture from her shop for Grandfather's condo. Furnishing it, or staging, you called it, Anjelica, when he first looked at the place."

"That's right. All I knew at the time was that the buyer came from China. So, I designed the interior of the condo in what I hoped would be pleasing—make him feel at home."

"I guess your efforts paid off," Stan said.

"They sure did. Grandfather walked in, and that was it," Charlie said.

"We designers call it staging, Mr. Wurthy. Helps to sell the property." Jeli chuckled, a nervous chuckle. The tension between father and son transferred to her every time she spoke.

She was relieved to hear the doorbell, thankful she didn't have to say more about Mr. Wu, or was it her imagination. It didn't matter what the reason, the tension was real, filling her with apprehension for the rest of her visit.

"Ah, that's the pizza. I thought we could sit here by the fire. Charles, will you get the plates, napkins on the counter, while I pay the delivery boy?"

"Sure can."

Charlie went to the kitchen, Stan to the front door. Jeli took the opportunity to stroll around the room. There were two floor-to-ceiling bookcases, the shelves filled with books. Checking the titles along the spines, most appeared to be about business—investing, management, personnel, marketing. But the bulk of the subjects were on financial management. A few pictures were tucked between the books—men at a conference table grinning at the camera, men shaking hands with other men. Mr. Wurthy appeared in all of the photos.

Stepping to the warmth of the fireplace, Jeli glanced at the candlesticks on the mantel, devoid of candles, her eyes moving along.

Her eyes froze.

Her heart stopped, then began thumping in her chest.

A chess piece, the emperor.

She picked it up for a closer look.

She had to be sure her eyes weren't playing tricks.

They weren't.

The chess piece was identical to the emperor in the set Jeli had staged on the island of Mr. Wu's condo. A chill ran up her arms.

She struggled to breathe.

"Come, sit, Ms. Bradley, while the pizza is hot."

With a shaky hand, Jeli put the emperor back on the mantel and turned to Mr. Wurthy. He was staring at her, his eyes piercing hers, daring her...daring her to do what? Her mind sparked in all directions.

Did he see her staring at the piece? Of course he did.

What were the chances Mr. Wurthy had the same piece from another set?

It was the only chess piece she saw in the room.

The piece put him at the scene...in the condo.

Oh, my God—did he kill Mr. Wu?

Charlie ambled back into the room, set three plates, forks, and napkins on the coffee table. He pulled up an ottoman, sat down, his back to the fireplace.

Mr. Wurthy set the pizza box on the table, lifted the lid. The scent of pepperoni and mushrooms circled their noses.

"Come on, Ms. Bradley, join us."

Jeli concentrated on her legs, making them move. She walked slowly to the couch, sat facing Charlie, trying to find her voice. "It smells divine. Charlie, a little wine please." She lifted a wedge of pizza, took a bite. "Umm, it's delicious. You have to give me the name of the pizza shop this came from," she said, smiling sweetly at Mr. Wurthy.

His body seemed to relax as she smiled.

I have to get out.

But how?

What excuse?

Shoe. I have to call Shoe.

No. The emperor is from another set, an identical set. No. No it's not. But if it is from Mr. Wu's set, how did he get it? He was only at the condo a few minutes, came and went...as I remember. The chess set was scattered on the floor. I didn't see him bend over. But he could have. You're letting your mind do cartwheels for nothing. Still...

Jeli carefully set her glass down on the coffee table, carefully picked up her napkin, carefully wiped her mouth, then suddenly bent over clutching her stomach. "Charlie, I think I'd better leave. My stomach doesn't feel so good...I need some air..."

Not waiting for an answer, she got up, stumbled to the hall, grabbed her coat.

"I'm sorry, Mr. Wurthy...dinner another time. Charlie, please, I think I'm going to be sick."

"Not a problem. I only hope you can sleep it off. It's been an emotional day. I'll be back, Dad, Save me some pizza."

"I will, son. I trust you'll be okay, Ms. Bradley?"

"I'm sure I will. Bye," she said darting out the door.

Charlie grabbed her arm as she slipped on a piece of ice. "Easy, easy. Don't worry I'll get you home in a jiffy."

On the way to the apartment, Jeli bent forward, faking a stomach cramp. "Just drop me off, Charlie. I'm going to run up."

"Okay. I'll call in the morning. Thanks again for today...introducing me to Faye."

"Sure, sure."

Jeli darted from the car, up the steps, fumbled for the key, pressed the buzzer instead.

"Susan, it's me. Let me in."

The lock clicked.

Taking the stairs two at a time, Jeli ran into the apartment slamming the door shut, leaned back against the door gasping for air.

Chapter 43

———

A SHADOWY FIGURE STOOD outside the circular illumination of the streetlight, eyes raised to the window on the fourth floor of the brick apartment building.

The lamp in the window silhouetted a woman. The woman was pacing, back and forth, in and out of the lamp's light.

The light in the window went out.

The shadowy figure across the street moved on, disappearing in the thick falling snow.

Chapter 44

———

SUSAN KNOCKED TWICE. "Jeli, you awake?"

"Yep. Come in." Jeli pulled back the edge of the quilt, welcoming Susan to climb in.

"Jeli, I've been thinking about what you told me when you got home...the chess piece. You should call Detective Shoe *now*. If Mr. Wurthy feels threatened...the way he looked at you, with daggers you said, when you held the chess piece...well, let's just say, you could be in danger. If he killed Mr. Wu, then he could very likely kill again to protect himself."

"I know. But do you mean I should call *now*? It's almost midnight."

"Do you have his cell? Or is it a work number? You could text him. Either way, I think you have to alert him to your suspicions," Susan said.

"What if I'm wrong? He may not be involved at all."

"There's only one way to find out, and Shoe is the person to follow the lead."

"You're right. Hand me my cell. It's on the table by you." Jeli could feel her heartbeat spike just thinking about telling the detective. She took a deep breath. "I'll text him. That way he can get back to me on his own time. Calling is so intrusive, especially at this time of night. I hate calls after I'm in bed. Don't you?"

"They scare me," Susan said fluffing up the pillow against the headboard, leaned back, then leaned forward watching Jeli type the text. In the pitch black room, their faces glowed in the light of the phones display.

Hi detective. Had dinner with Mr. Wurthy & son. Startled to see chess piece, emperor, same as Wu's. Is emperor missing? A connection? Jeli

"There. Whatta you think? Any changes?" Jeli said.

"Send it. I'll feel better. Maybe then we can get some sleep," Susan said, climbing out of the bed.

Suddenly the Saints marched. Susan jumped back in the bed, putting her ear to Jeli's as she answered.

"Hi, Detective. I didn't expect to hear—"

"Where exactly did you see this emperor? In Mr. Stan Wurthy's house—"

"In the living room, on the fireplace mantel."

"Did you pick it up?"

"Yes…oh, fingerprints. But mine would be on the piece because I set it up. It's an old set, so there could be lots of fingerprints, if that's what you thinking."

"Okay. Come to the department in the morning. We'll fingerprint you and pull off any other prints for the file. Maybe it's not the one-and-the-same emperor," Shoe said with a chuckle "Did Mr. Wurthy see you pick it up?"

"Yes, and it was spooky, I mean the way he looked, like he caught me in the act of something bad. Of course, I wasn't guilty of anything except to pick up the piece. But I felt unnerved, no, I suddenly felt panicky. I wanted to run. All I could think was to make up an excuse so Charlie could take me home."

"Umm, Charlie. I'll need to fingerprint him too and—"

"Oh, I don't think Charlie—"

"You never know, Ms. Bradley."

"He's never been to my roommate's apartment—wait, he handled a framed picture on Faye Yoon's desk. I think I could borrow it from her. I could say I wanted to make a copy of the picture for Charlie. I'll wear gloves, after all it is cold outside."

Susan giggled at Jeli's drama-queen act. Jeli returned a wide-eye stare, shrugging her shoulders.

"Sounds good, Ms. Bradley. Pick up the frame before you come to see me. In the meantime, I'll check the chess set in the box of Mr. Wu's belongings. And, Ms. Bradley, if...if the emperor is missing, if we find a connection, watch yourself. Doors locked. I'll put your building on the night cruiser's surveillance route. See you tomorrow. What time does Ms. Faye Yoon open the store?"

"Nine, I think. She lives above the shop."

"After I give the frame to the lab, I have to visit Billy Qiáng again. He doesn't have an alibi and he obviously had the opportunity."

Chapter 45

———

THE SOUNDS OF SNOWPLOWS scraping the pavement ripped through Jeli's dream. Bolting upright, her breathing returned to normal, eyes trained on the bedroom window. It had stopped snowing.

Sighing, she climbed out of bed, slipping her feet into the kittens. She shook her head, freeing her mind of Stan Wurthy's sinister face glaring down on her. "Shoe's probably right—a big *if* that's the emperor...stop it, Anjelica Jane. You have appointments today," she muttered, admonishing herself to get a move on.

Jeli padded to the kitchen, following the scent of fresh brewed coffee. Susan was sitting at the table sipping from her mug, gazing at the window. She looked up as Jeli poured her coffee. Neither said anything, waiting for the jolt of caffeine. Mug in hand, Jeli looked through the lace curtain covering the kitchen window. The sun's rays were brilliant bouncing off the crystals of new snow.

"It's a beautiful day," Jeli said.

"Umm," Susan replied.

Jeli smiled. "Thank God for the sunshine, chasing away stupid thoughts of emperors...chess sets."

"They weren't stupid, Jeli."

"Maybe not. Thanks for the coffee. I have to get going. First, I'll call Faye. Being Sunday, I want to make sure she's going to be open, or at least let me pick up the frame."

"I'm going to pop into work for a few hours. Give me call if you think you'll be back for dinner," Susan said.

"Will do." Between sips of coffee, Jeli showered, dressed, thought about what she was going to say to Faye. With the meeting scheduled with Shoe, and another visit with Qiáng, she decided it was not a good time to talk to Faye about her life's plan. Besides she was still too unsettled from last night at the Wurthy's to have a casual conversation about life. Placing the call to Faye, she made an excuse that she was seeing Charlie soon and wanted to make a copy of the picture on her desk, framing it as a gift. Faye, told her to come ahead, ten-ish. She had a special appointment with a client, so she couldn't chat.

Getting off the bus, Jeli breathed in the fresh air, and began the short trek to Faye's shop. Suddenly, she felt a chill up her arm. She stopped at a shop window, her eyes scanning the reflection. Was someone watching her? A couple passed, holding hands, laughing. A car passed. Sighing, she picked up her pace. Faye's shop was a few doors away.

As it happened, Faye's customer, a family trying to decide on a living-room set, was in an animated conversation with the shopkeeper. Faye had wrapped the five-by-seven inch picture in a plastic bag. Jeli was in and out in a couple of minutes, whispering thank you and I'll see you soon, as she made her exit.

Chapter 46

———

DOWN THE STREET FROM Yoon's shop, Jeli stopped mid-stride to call Shoe, alert him that she had the picture frame and was on her way to the precinct to meet him. He told her to wait in front of the bookstore, he and his partner would pick her up in the black and white.

Jeli strode down to The Story Teller bookstore. Within minutes, she was settled in the backseat of the squad car, headed to the condo and the appointment with Billy Qiáng.

"Anything on the emperor chess piece, Detective? Was it with the evidence you guys picked up?" Jeli said. She was leaning forward, gazing at the array of gadgets embedded in the dash. "Man-oh-man, do you really know what all those buttons trigger?"

"Sure do, Ms. Bradley. High-end communications," Officer Stewart said, grinning.

"Nothing on the chess piece," Shoe said. "It's Sunday, short staff, a wild weekend of bookings. We'll know tomorrow."

Leaning her head between the two officers, Jeli said, "I remembered something else, after we talked last night, Detective. When I met Mr. Wu, the first time he came to view the condo, both Josh and I noticed a gold ring on his middle finger, right hand. It was very thick. Of course, he was a pudgy man, and his fingers were large. The ring seemed extra large and had a big diamond mounted in the center. After Mr. Wu left with Billy, Josh commented, that with the price of gold these days, the ring was very valuable."

"I don't think I saw a ring on his fingers. With your description, I should have," Officer Stewart said.

"That's just it, it occurred to me last night, that the ring wasn't on his finger when the doctor examined him. I remember because the doc raised Wu's hand and made the comment that it was stiff, rigor mortis setting in."

"Okay. We have two items to search for and a particular question I want to ask Billy when we go through the condo again this morning. Stewart, you start the search while Ms. Bradley and I question Billy. Ms. Bradley, you stay with me, but I do want you to take another walk through—see if you notice anything else amiss."

Shoe pulled to the curb of the condo building. Officer Stewart hopped out to open the door for Jeli. She hurried ahead in her fashion boots, purple scarf fanning out as she pushed the buzzer for Billy to let them in.

Back by the car, Stewart whispered to his boss, "Ms. Bradley sure is beautiful...and that hair." A soft whistle punctuated his remark.

With a sharp glare from his boss, Stewart wiped away the smile on his face, falling in behind Shoe to the front entrance.

Chapter 47

———

THE ELEVATOR JERKED TO a stop at the fourth floor. With a soft ding, the door slid open. Billy Qiáng stood in the condo's open doorway, arms crossed over his broad chest. A lesser person might have pressed the button marked down, not wanting to tangle with the large man. But Jeli didn't see anger, only fear in his eyes. She walked toward him, her hand extended.

"Hello, Billy."

"Ms. Bradley." He nodded, gently accepting her delicate hand in his.

"Good to see you," she said, threading her arm through Billy's as they went inside.

Detective Shoe and Officer Stewart followed, Stewart closing the door behind them.

The detective laid a tablet on the island, glanced around.

"Billy, I've asked my partner to take another look around. Since I took your initial statement, a few questions have come up, questions I hope you can help me with."

Billy stood mute, once again his arms crossing his chest.

"Stewart, you go ahead. We'll stay here in the living room. Ms. Bradley, Billy, please take a seat."

Jeli and Billy sat side by side on the couch as Shoe picked up his tablet, then sat on a side chair by the coffee table.

"Billy, since the last time we looked around, the day Mr. Wu died, have you found any chess pieces? They were scattered on the floor if you recall?"

"No, sir. You, or...the other officer...someone picked up all the pieces."

"Well, there was the piece in the birdcage, a small piece I'd call a pawn."

"We call the small pieces soldiers. Mr. Wu trained Chang-ying to pick up small things...a button, a piece of bird food. He fetched things, taking them to his cage, sometimes dropping them places."

"So, you haven't found a piece—around the kitchen, a window sill?"

"No, sir. But I haven't looked either."

"Excuse me, Detective. I found this in Mr. Qiáng's top dresser drawer, in the toe of a sock," Stewart said, handing a large gold ring with a diamond to Shoe.

Shoe examined the ring Stewart put in the palm of his hand, looked at Jeli, her mouth gaped open, brows raised. "Is this the ring you saw Mr. Wu wearing, Ms. Bradley?"

"Yes...yes, it is." Jeli looked up at Billy, his face blank. She was sure the detective was wondering if Billy was telling the truth, or did he pocket the ring after he killed him? A shiver ran down her spine at the thought. She certainly didn't know him well enough to say, but he seemed like a scared cuddly bear at the moment.

"Billy, why did you hide Mr. Wu's ring in your drawer? Clearly, if you put it in one of your socks you didn't want us to find it."

"He...he gave it to me."

"But Ms. Bradley saw it on his finger."

"He gave it to me after we boarded the plane in Beijing...the last time. He said it was mine now. He gave it to me in payment for my loyalty. He said if things changed, I could sell it for a new start in America."

"What did he mean, 'if things changed?'"

"I don't know. He just said it. I could never wear such a valuable ring...I was afraid it would be stolen. That's why I put it in my sock. Please, please, don't take it. It's all I have."

"I'm sorry, Billy. I have to take it for now. It may be evidence. If, or when, it is not found to be material to the case, it will be returned to you. When Mr. Wu gave it to you, did he give you a note, saying it was a gift? Did he sign anything?"

"No, no, he just took it off, laid it in my hand."

"Billy, I have another question. Do you have any idea why Mr. Wu was found so far from his wheelchair?"

Shoe stood walked with long strides to the wheelchair by the fireplace. He turned and strode to the bedroom doorway. "There are several yards from the wheelchair to this door."

"I...I don't know," Billy said, stammering.

"You told me before that Mr. Wu couldn't walk, or that you had never seen him walk. If he crawled...before he took his last breath...there must have been a strong reason. Wu was dying. Why was it so important to get into the bedroom? Was he after something?"

"I don't know. I don't know. The only thing in his bedroom is his case."

"What's in this case that's so valuable?"

"I don't know. I never saw...he never said."

"Where is this...case?"

"The second drawer of his dresser."

Chapter 48

———

SHOE STARED AT THE BIG MAN.

"You would do well to help us, Billy. Stop holding back information. Show us this case."

Billy stared back at the detective, diverted his eyes to Jeli. She nodded—*do what the detective asks.*

With a sigh, Billy reluctantly stepped to the bedroom. Detective Shoe and Officer Stewart followed. Standing in front of the dresser, Billy shook his head. "Mr. Wu asked me to put the case in this drawer because he could open it from his wheelchair. He didn't want anyone to know it existed...made me promise under no circumstances was I to tell Charlie. He never said what was inside."

"Mr. Wu is dead, Billy. He was murdered. If the contents of the case points to the killer, you have to show us."

Billy looked up, as if asking Mr. Wu to forgive him. Pulling on the knobs, he opened the drawer revealing a shiny silver case, the size of a large briefcase, about five inches deep.

Shoe lifted the case out of the drawer, setting it on the bed.

Jeli leaned against the doorframe watching the two officers and Billy. Billy stood defiantly—feet apart, arms over his chest, fear remaining in his eyes.

The case was locked.

"Billy, do you have a key? Know where Mr. Wu might have put a key?"

Billy shook his head.

Shoe looked at his partner. "Take this to the car and open it— do whatever you have to do and bring it back here."

Stewart picked up the heavy steel case, carrying it down in the elevator, out to the squad car.

Jeli, the detective, and Billy returned to the living room. "Any bottled water, Billy?" Jeli said.

Billy didn't reply. He walked to the refrigerator, returning with three bottles of water. He handed one to the detective, one to Jeli, and unscrewed the cap of one for himself.

Silence filled the room.

Jeli was sure she heard her heart beat. She looked around, sipping the water. "Detective, that Buddha on the mantel, I don't remember seeing it before."

Shoe looked over at the mantel. "Billy. Do you know where that statue came from?"

"I gave it to Mr. Wu the day Charlie brought us here, dropped us off, the first night we slept here...the day before..."

Billy choked, unable to finish the sentence.

Shoe sighed, took a sip of water, then walked to the fireplace. Pulling his handkerchief from his pants pocket, he lifted the statue made of heavy bronze.

The three jerked together at the muffled sound of a gunshot.

Stewart returned setting the steel case on the kitchen island. He looked at Shoe.

Shoe nodded. The bullet shot out the lock.

Stewart lifted the lid.

Inside the case was a stack of papers. Shoe glanced at several of the sheets. "Seems to be full of letters, all marked COPY at the bottom."

The detective took the letters, returning to the chair by the coffee table, and began to read. He paused, leaning back in the chair. "Ms. Bradley, please read this letter out loud, it appears to be the oldest."

Jeli sat cross legged at the coffee table, taking the sheets of paper from the detective's hand. Swallowing a sip of water, bending her head forward, she began to read the two-page letter.

Chapter 49

———

August 19, 1983

To: Mr. Stan Wurthy

As you well know, my wife and daughter were killed one week ago today in an automobile accident. Also, as you well know by now, I suffered a spinal injury in the same accident leaving me a cripple. The doctors say I probably will never walk again. They gave me a glimmer of hope that with an operation, one or more, and therapy, there is a slight chance I will recover from the injury to my legs.

Also as you know, the accident happened the day you were to marry my daughter Amy, in fact my wife and I were driving Amy to meet you for the ceremony.

Also as you know, Amy gave birth to your son in Boston six months ago. You and Amy named him Charles.

As I write this letter, baby Charles is being cared for by friends who live on a nearby farm.

Also as you know, you visited me two days after the accident in the hospital. You were with the police, and the police told me I was lucky to be alive, but that they have not been able to find the driver who hit me, and that if they do, the person will be arrested and charged with manslaughter. After examining the scene, they believe it was not an accident—the driver was speeding, maybe drunk, no skid marks showing that the driver tried to brake, or that the driver attempted to veer away. The police said, unless the driver can show otherwise, it was not an accident. It was intentional.

All this you know.

Now for what you don't know.

I saw the driver of the car that killed my wife and daughter.

You were that driver!

Now, as I see it, I have two very simple choices. I can tell the police it was you, or I don't tell the police it was you.

The first choice, while giving me satisfaction, satisfaction is all I gain, and baby Charlie loses his father to the firing squad, loses his wealthy father.

The second choice, leave the accident as just that—hit and run, although I would imagine you suffered some injury before you made your getaway. I marvel that the car you were driving was still running—but yours was a very big car. Mine no bigger than a rickshaw.

Here is what I ask to keep silent, to keep a secret I will take to my grave.

I ask for a settlement—fifty thousand dollars (in Yuan). With the money Charlie and I will leave the farm, set up housekeeping in Beijing, and I will invest in a laundry business.

Oh, yes, Charlie. You can be part of the boy's life or not. Your choice.

The nurse has given me an envelope in which I will put this letter and seal it. You said you would visit me today. I will give you the letter. Ask you to read it, and say you accept. There can be no other answer. If you say no, I will

make a big fuss, yelling that you are trying to kill me—
much like your fake sorrow over the fact that Amy is dead.

Also, I am writing a duplicate of this letter for my
safekeeping.

You have one hour to tell me if we have a deal at which
time you will tell me when I can expect the settlement, but
no longer than two weeks away.
Wu, Grandfather of baby Charles Wurthy.
COPY

Chapter 50

———

SHOE CLEARED HIS THROAT.

Officer Stewart helped himself to a bottle of water from the fridge.

Jeli's eyes slid from Billy to the detective, as she handed the letters back to him.

Shoe laid the letter face down on the coffee table, then rifled through the remaining sheets of paper changing the order.

"Ms. Bradley, please read a few more. They're short, a few paragraphs each," Shoe said handing her the letters.

> *August 15, 1991*
>
> *Charlie enjoyed visiting you in Boston. I agree he should be schooled in America. I believe you call it grade school. He would attend third grade?*
>
> *Boarding school seems a bit lonely, but you can give it a try. I want him home over your holidays, and, of course, summer vacation.*
>
> *I'm a bit short this month. Please send $500. Also send the plane tickets to Boston, two round trips. One is for a neighbor who will travel with Charlie. My neighbor plans to stay with family in New York until school lets out, at which time he'll accompany Charlie back to Beijing.*
> *Wu Chao*
> *COPY*
>
> *April 10, 2004*

Charlie told me he's doing well at college, graduating in another month, and wants to live permanently in the States. He's twenty-one, so I guess it's time to let him make up his own mind.

I'm running very short of money and I want to pay off the loan I took out on the laundry plus other bills.

Send wire transfer as before to my bank: $2000.
Wu Chao
COPY

November 2015

I borrowed, you call it buying on margin, to buy a sure winner in the Shanghai stock market.

Wire $5000 immediately. The market is going crazy up. The government is urging us all to participate in the market. If it keeps on the present track, I may not have to ask for more funds in the future.
Wu Chao
COPY

"Well, things seem to be turning around for Mr. Wu," Detective Shoe said. "Ms. Bradley, read the last three letters if you please."

Jeli chugged the last of her water, cleared her throat, and began to read.

January 9, 2016

Things aren't good. Market plunged. I'm liquidating what I can before I lose all. I'm going to buy property in Boston to be near Charlie and friends. Will visit soon. Staying with Charlie. Wire transfer $5000 to cover my visit.

Wu Chao
COPY

February 4, 2016

Made decision on property. Having trouble with stock market. Require $10,000 to cover short position. Charlie helped me open bank account in Boston. Attached is the account number.

WIRE TODAY TO NEW ACCOUNT!!
Wu Chao
COPY

February 17, 2016

I lost everything —all money in market, more than likely my laundry. Need $15,000 for down payment on Boston condo. WIRE transfer to Boston account. Will arrive in two days.
Wu Chao
COPY

Chapter 51

———

AS JELI LAID THE last letter face down on the others, Shoe snapped to his feet, strode out in the hallway by the elevator. "I have to make a call. Ms. Bradley, put the letters back in the case. Everybody stay put. I'll be right back."

Jeli picked up the letters, evened the sheets of paper, and returned them to the case, shut the lid. Sitting on the chair Shoe had vacated, she slipped off her fashion boots, wiggled her toes, flexed her feet in their green argyle socks. She felt Billy and Officer Stewart eyeing her, watching every move as if in a trance. She smiled, returning her feet into the cramped fashion statement.

"Okay, here's what's going to happen," Shoe said, as he approached the living room. "Billy, given what you said this morning, I've arranged for an officer to pick you up, take you to the precinct to give your statement for the record. Stewart, you are to stay with Billy—fingerprint him, lead the questioning. Billy, you will be free to go once Officer Stewart is satisfied he has everything. But you are not to leave the city or you'll face arrest. Do you understand?"

"Yes, sir."

"I'm leaving now to drop off the new pieces of evidence at the lab and will take Ms. Bradley to her apartment. Any questions?"

Everyone shook their heads.

"Good. Ms. Bradley, let's go. You take the statue in the evidence bag. I have the ring and the case."

Jeli patted Billy's shoulder on the way out, picked up the statue and headed for the elevator.

"Stewart, call me if you have anything new," Shoe said, as he followed Jeli to the elevator.

———

FINISHED WITH HIS INSTRUCTIONS to the lab tech, and Jeli fingerprinted, Shoe, with his passenger, climbed into the squad car to drive to her apartment.

"Seatbelt, Ms. Bradley."

"You sound like my brother."

"I've met Marshall. Smart man. He gave a seminar to my officers on how to detect a cyber attack."

"You're barking up the wrong tree, you know," Jeli said gazing out the car window at the dirty snow banks. She loved the seasons, but disliked the dregs of winter.

"What tree is that, Ms. Bradley?"

"Billy Qiáng. He could never have killed, Mr. Wu. He loved him, treated with tenderness."

"What makes you think that's what I'm thinking?" Shoe said.

"Oh, taking him in, fingerprinting him, scaring the heck out of him."

"Good police work, Ms. Bradley. Can't get tunnel vision. Can't let your emotions take over an investigation or all of a sudden you're definitely 'barking up the wrong tree.'"

Jeli turned in her seat, straining against the belt, fixing her eyes on the detective.

Shoe checked his mirror, set his turn signal and made a left turn onto her street.

"Stan Wurthy should be your prime suspect. He was being blackmailed big time, from what we read in Mr. Wu's letters. And, don't forget, he said he was facing bankruptcy. A person can only be pushed so far—they snap."

"You want to join the force, Ms. Bradley?"

"No, just saying. Being a police woman is not in my game plan." Jeli turned away, looked out her window again. "Of course, one can always change course."

"I'm assigning an officer to stay with you for a few hours, maybe a couple of days. I hope she won't inconvenience you and your roommate too much."

"Good heavens, why?"

"A precaution. I've never been accused of tunnel vision, and I don't plan to fall into that trap at this stage of my career."

"Talk about tunnel vision, Detective. If you're looking at Billy, how about Josh Greely. He has keys to the building—every door."

"Umm. Anyway, you saw something and it's possible a certain person witnessed you picking it up, examining it and—"

"The chess piece...the emperor?"

"Could be."

"It's not necessary, Detective. With two older brothers and a crime-reporter sister, I've been trained to evade and survive. Thanks, but no thanks."

"Well, don't go out unless you let me know. You'll be on a fifteen-minute drive by until we can bring the suspect in...not saying who."

"Okay, but I bet I know who that is—"

"Tunnel vision, Ms. Bradley. Don't be so sure."

"That's my building on the right."

"I know, Ms. Bradley. Thanks for coming along today. Don't hesitate to call me if you need help...even if you think it's nothing."

"I will, Detective. Thanks for the lift."

———

SHOE PULLED AWAY FROM the curb after Jeli disappeared into the building. He activated the squad car's communication panel.

"Stewart, Shoe here. Ms. Bradley is in her apartment. Did you get the search warrant for the Wurthy house?"

"It's in the works. I'll serve it personally within the hour. I called the lab. They hope to have the results for you tonight, but no later than early morning—3:00 or 4:00 a.m."

"Did you instruct the lab tech to call me, no matter the time?"

"Yes, I did."

"How's it going with Billy?"

"All done. He's on his way back to the condo. He's a little spooked—may get a room somewhere. I told him to be sure and let me know—threatened him again if he decided to leave the city he'd be arrested. He definitely got the message."

"Okay. Let me know when you bring in Stan Wurthy, serve the search warrant. Take the chess piece to the lab right away. And one more thing, bring in Josh Greely. Fingerprint him, and get his statement on the record."

"Roger that."

Chapter 52

———

THE CLOUDS FINALLY DRIFTED north to Maine, on to Nova Scotia, leaving a bright moonlit night. It was eleven o'clock. Every time Jeli closed her eyes, they popped open with yet another image of Mr. Wu's blackmail letters, of Billy's eyes filling with tears. The big man fought back mightily, trying not to let them roll down his cheeks.

Punching the pillow, Jeli laid her head back down, staring at the ceiling. While the detective didn't actually say he was going to the Wurthy house to collect the chess piece, she was pretty sure that was his aim to do so. Maybe right now, as she was lying safe in her bed, Stan Wurthy was being arrested.

Her eyes slid to the clock on her nightstand. 11:06.

The Saints began their march, scaring her half to death.

It was Josh.

Oh my God, maybe Shoe arrested him because of what she said—he had a key, keys to the whole building. Why didn't I keep my big mouth shut? Maybe he'll hang up if I don't answer.

The Saints marched for the third time.

"Hi, Josh. What's up?"

"THAT'S what I want to know! Did you tell that Detective Shoe and his boys that I had a key to Wu's unit?"

Josh was yelling, and getting louder with each word.

"Well—" She wasn't going to admit she might have hinted that he had keys. But she didn't have to lie because Josh kept on ranting.

"His goons picked me up like a common criminal. The one night I stayed with my dad, and this happens."

"Where are you now—in jail?" Jeli said in as calm a voice she could muster. He was scaring her, her chest heaving, up and down.

"No, I'm not in jail! Two hours they questioned me. Two stupid hours. I'm at my dad's trying to calm him down. He says I'm ruining his reputation. He ordered me out of the house again. Can you beat that? Well, this time I told him I'm staying put. No more mattress on the floor—no sir. Just thinking about it makes me feel like a jailbird."

"It's probably a good idea...to stay at home until the police solve the case...it might look suspicious if they knew you were staying next door to Wu...you know, like easy access."

"Red, what are you saying? You think I killed the old guy? I certainly wanted to when his check bounced."

"Calm down, Josh. If they suspected you...they wouldn't have let you go...unless—"

"Unless what? Never mind. Because of Wu screwing me, I'm late on the bank payment."

Jeli heard his sigh.

He stopped yelling. Maybe this was her opportunity to reiterate that she might branch out, drum up new clients.

"Let me know when things settle for you, Josh, when you begin renovating the other units. Until then...I'll work with some new clients. I have bills to pay, too, you know."

"Sure, whatever."

The phone went dead. Josh had hung up.

As if she wasn't unsettled enough, his yelling had made it worse. Well, that's the end of any romantic thoughts about Mr. Josh Greely.

Climbing out of bed, she padded on bare feet to the window. A black and white squad car rolled by.

"Great, just great. I could be bound with duct tape and they'd just keep rolling along," she muttered.

Grabbing her pillow, she tiptoed to Susan's door, knocked softly.

"Susan? You awake? Susan?"

"Jeli?"

"Yep. You awake?"

"I am now. Come on in." Susan pulled back her blanket, patted the sheet. "What's the matter can't sleep?"

Jeli climbed up on the bed, fluffing her pillow against the headboard.

"Josh just called. He was yelling at me that he'd been picked up for questioning."

"No wonder you can't sleep after you told me about today. Scrunch down, see if you can relax. We both need some shut eye. I have to demo my program to the staff in the morning."

"Thanks." Jeli stared at the ceiling. "Susan, maybe I should go back to the farm—city life is scary." Jeli said, pulling the blanket up.

Susan didn't answer.

No more girl talk tonight.

Chapter 53

———

THE BROWN LEATHER COUCH was worn, cracked in places, but the price at Goodwill was doable. Shoe was always thankful on nights like this that he had sprung for it on his own dime. When he was promoted to head the Criminal Investigation Division of his precinct, he knew he would pull some all-nighters.

All aspects of the Wu murder case were spiraling at the same time. He felt in his gut that the next few hours were crucial and he wasn't going to waste a minute going home, only to be called back. No, he was staying put in his office waiting for information from the lab, waiting for Stewart to report he had Stan Wurthy in custody.

It was 2:13 a.m. by his watch. Grabbing a small pillow from the bottom drawer of his desk, he stepped to the couch. Tossing the pillow at one end, he laid his weary body down, his cell clasped in his hands, resting on his stomach.

The detective's breathing eased into a light sleep.

It could have been hours, but only eight minutes had passed when his cell rang.

It was the lab.

"Harry, give it to me," Shoe said.

"I just sent my report to you. Should be in your inbox," the lab tech said.

Shoe was on his feet, quickly stepped to his computer, clicking icons to gain access to the lab report.

"Give me an overview while I open the file." Shoe said.

"Okay…from the top. The chess set in the evidence bag—no king—"

"Emperor."

"Whatever—it's missing. Officer Stewart called. There wasn't any chess piece on Wurthy's fireplace mantel."

"What? Ms. Bradley said—"

"Officer Stewart said there was no king, emperor, whatever, chess piece on the mantel. And yes, to your next question, he said he scoured the house. Nothing. And no, to your follow-up question, Stan Wurthy was not home and no car in the garage."

"Wait. Do you know if Wurthy was picked up?"

"As far as I know, he hasn't been."

"Hold on, Stewart's calling. Stewart, what's going on? Harry's on hold. He said you didn't find the chess piece. Where's Wurthy?"

"Roger the chess piece. An officer and I looked everywhere. No Wurthy and no car. I'd say he's on the run."

"We already have an APB out on him. For God's sake, double your efforts…and keep me posted." Shoe cut the call, switching back to the lab tech.

"Stewart repeated what you told me, Harry. Okay, back to your report. What about the Buddha statue—prints, blood?"

"First the prints. There were several. No matches except for one—Billy Qiáng. Now, as for the statue itself, it could be the murder weapon. The blow on the head of Mr. Wu, in the morgue, was caused by a blunt instrument—same size as the statue and there is a trace of blood on the statue that matches Mr. Wu's. There is evidence that someone tried to wipe the statue but it was haphazard, leaving some partial prints, and, as I said, a trace of blood. No hair."

"If you get word that Stan Wurthy is in custody, get his prints ASAP. If there's no match on any of the items with his, then I'm afraid I'm back to square one."

"Except for Billy Qiáng," Harry said.

"What about Josh Greely? Any matches?"

"No. I dusted the bagged steel case you dropped off. The only prints on it came from Wu and Qiáng. "

"Qiáng? He said he touched it, put it in the drawer in the first place. I imagine Qiáng's prints are on the ring and, of course, Mr.

Wu's. Good work, Harry. Let me know the minute you have Stan's Wurthy's prints."

Shoe slapped his cell down on his desk, continuing to stare at the report on the screen. His eyes slid to the bottom right. 3:10 a.m. Too early to call Ms. Bradley. Stan Wurthy was his prime suspect and Officer Stewart hadn't brought him in yet. Shoe hadn't ruled out Qiáng, but his gut told him he didn't do it.

Shoe put his computer in sleep mode, and went back to the leather couch. He was out the minute his head hit the little pillow.

Chapter 54

———

JELI FELT LIKE A CAGED animal. Susan left for work, so there was no one to talk to. She couldn't call Pops, or her mom. They'd know in a millisecond that something was wrong. Same for Marshall, and, oh my God, Sadie and Travis would call out the National Guard. She looked at the empty coffee pot—she'd already had too much caffeine. Her nerves were on high alert as it was. Peering out the window at the street below, another squad car rolled by.

Thank God, the saints were marching. She didn't recognize the caller ID. Maybe it was a new client. 9:30 was a respectable time to call.

"Hello," Jeli said.

"Is this Ms. Bradley?"

"Yes it is."

"We haven't met. You come highly recommended…ah…"

"I'm sorry, can you speak up. I can barely hear you."

"There is a Chinese client who wants to see the condo you did the interior design for. But he's leaving for China. Only has an hour. He really wants to see the property…now…10:15…he'll be there."

"I don't have a key," Jeli said.

"I do," the caller said.

"Okay. I can be there in twenty minutes. Ask your client to please wait, Mr. …what's your name?" The call was disconnected.

Finally, she had something to do. Something productive.

Jeli called for an Uber as she hopped around slipping on her fashion boots.

Susan was at work and she didn't want to interrupt her so she sent her a text. *Leaving for showing at condo. Talk tonight.*

Five minutes later she dashed out of the building and into the waiting Uber taxi.

Chapter 55

——

DETECTIVE SHOE CHECKED WITH the lab and Officer Stewart again. He received the same story—no sign of Stan Wurthy.

It was almost ten o'clock.

Time to check in with Ms. Bradley.

She didn't pick up her cell. *Maybe she was in the shower*, he thought frowning.

"Ms. Bradley, Detective Shoe here. Stan Wurthy seems to have disappeared. Keep your door locked. Don't go out unless you call me first. I'll let you know when we have him in custody."

Chapter 56

———

A COLD AIR MASS DROPPED down from Canada chasing any thoughts of spring away, leaving New England in a deep freeze. A wind chill of minus five degrees was breaking records from Maine south to Massachusetts. Bundled deep in her parka, fur around the hood, each breath released a puff of white crystals.

Jeli paid the Uber driver, and made a dash for the condo building. Pressing the buzzer for 4A, an immediate click unlocked the front door.

Squashing her inner voice ringing in her ears that said she should have asked for the realtor's name. She tried but the caller had hung up.

Stepping out of the elevator, she relaxed hearing soothing music, *Send in the Clowns,* through the open door. Maybe Faye was with the realtor and the new client.

Tension gone, Jeli smiled entering the condo.

"Hello, hello," she called out, unzipping her parka.

"Ms. Bradley, how prompt you are. Take your parka off, sit, while I close the door."

Jeli's body stiffened.

Terror filled her eyes.

Chapter 57

———

LINES OF CODE FLASHED on the screen as Susan scrolled down the computer file. Absentmindedly, she picked up her phone ringing on her desk, her eyes never leaving the computer screen.

"Susan Li," she said.

"Ah, Ms. Li. This is Detective Shoe. I'm trying to reach Ms. Bradley but she isn't picking up her cell. By any chance do you know where she is?"

"Oh, hi, Detective. Yes, she had a call from a realtor, another client from China. She must have left her phone in the apartment. She was in a hurry to—"

"Did she tell you the name of the realtor?"

"No. She sent a text message. I'm sure she was excited to think, that just maybe, the condo would sell after all, with a new prospect. Is something wrong, Detective? Your voice—"

"I'm not sure, Ms. Li, but you've been a big help. I'll go over to the condo. If Ms. Bradley calls you, please let her know I'm trying to reach her?"

"Yes, of course."

Chapter 58

———

THE MAN WAS CRAZED.

What do I do? Sadie, what do I do? Marshall?

Stan glared at Jeli, a gun in his hand, waving the revolver to the chair by the fireplace, telling her to sit in the chair. She did, anything to stop his waving the gun around.

"I was called to see...I didn't recognize your voice, or—"

"I know. Sorry for the little deception, but I found it quite necessary," Wurthy said.

Closing the door, he returned, the gun continually trained on Jeli.

Her eyes darted around the living room, the kitchen, the hall, looking for an escape route, looking for anything to distract him. "What's the matter with you, Mr. Wurthy? There must be some mistake, why did you call me? A misunderstanding?"

Jeli stood, snatched her parka, jammed her arms through the sleeves.

"Yes, a mistake. It was a stupid mistake to take the chess piece...take the emperor. I thought it was a rather symbolic souvenir. You must understand that Mr. Wu had been blackmailing me for years, but the knight has slain the emperor." Wurthy dug in his pants pocket, retrieving a folded piece of paper. He waved it at Jeli. "Here, here is the last letter. Well, I showed him. The emperor is dead. I am the new emperor."

"Whatever do you mean? The knight? A new emperor?" Don't just talk, do something, Jeli. The crystal ball on the coffee table...throw it at the window? Surely someone would call the police. Domestic violence...

Stan's head rolled back, convulsed with laughter. "Oh, Ms. Bradley, I saw it in your eyes when you picked up the piece, the emperor, on my mantel. I read your mind. I'm sure the police have checked Mr. Wu's belongings, found the emperor missing, if not, it's only a matter of time. You did tell the detective what you found didn't you?"

Jeli couldn't stop the quiver running down her back, through her veins.

Stan leered at her. "Ah, yes, you did. You really must learn to keep a blank face when you lie. But it doesn't matter. You see I crushed the poor emperor, crushed it to nothing but a small pile of dust, flushed the remains down the toilet—such a sad burial. So, it comes to she said, he said—you say it was there, I say it wasn't. But it will never come to trial, because I'll be long gone, as will you be...gone. One death, two deaths, it doesn't matter. I'll be out of the country, and you...well, the dead can't testify. The whole sorry story will become a cold case. Who cares about some Chinese tourist?"

A door slammed. Both Stan and Jeli looked up, their eyes darting to the front door.

Chapter 59

———

THE VIRTUAL TEST WAS skimming from one screen to the next. So far so good. No crashes, no frozen code. A few more lines of code and Susan would be ready to demo the software at the team meeting in a couple of hours.

She stood, stretched, but her eyes never wavered from her computer.

Her desk phone rang, her fingers automatically picking it up, automatically pressing the button to engage the call.

"Susan, Charlie Wurthy here. I'm trying to reach Anjelica. Do you—"

"She went to the condo. A realtor called with a client from China. Gosh, everyone is looking for her. Detective Shoe rang me a few minutes ago—he's looking for her, too."

"Okay. I'll run over. Thanks."

"Hold on, Charlie. I'll go with you. I work for Jeli's brother. Do you know his building?"

"Yes, Jeli told me you worked for him. Wait outside. I'll have the driver stop to pick you up. Ten minutes?"

"That's good. I want to see if she's okay."

"What are you talking about—see if she's okay?"

"I'll explain in the car. Bye."

Chapter 60

———

"WHAT'S THAT?

Someone coming?

Front door?" Stan whispered through clenched teeth.

He grabbed Jeli, swung her in front of him, twisting her arm behind her back, pressing the gun to her ear.

"Anybody there?" he called out. "Seems we may have company, Ms. Bradley. Whoever it is just bought you some time. Is there a back entrance?"

Jeli shook her head.

"You're lying again, Ms. Bradley. Of course, there is."

The front door banged open. Shoe stepped inside, gun drawn.

"Drop the gun, Wurthy. Step away from Ms. Bradley."

"I don't think so, Detective. She's my ticket out of here. You shoot me, you hit her first. Now move out of our way."

The elevator dinged, the door sliding back. Charlie stepped out followed by Susan.

Shoe shot a glance over his shoulder.

"Get back in the elevator—both of you," Shoe shouted.

Charlie stood frozen in the doorway, unable to move, seeing his dad pressing a gun barrel to Anjelica's head.

"Dad, what are you doing?"

"Your girlfriend and I were just leaving. Now step away from the door," Stan said, waving his gun, tightening his grip on Jeli's arm.

"I told you to drop the gun, Wurthy, now," Shoe said, inching forward.

"Well now, if you shoot you kill Ms. Bradley, and I kill you, Detective. Of course, if I shoot first—"

Stan pointed the gun at the detective inching closer, dragging Jeli with him. If you're not going to move, I guess I'll just have to shoot—"

Jeli whirled, kneed Wurthy in the crotch.

Shots rang out.

Detective Shoe dropped to the floor.

Wurthy dropped his gun screaming in pain, collapsing backward on the couch as Billy emerged from the hall leading to the back door. A gun in his hand, held steady with his other hand, he leaned against the wall, dropped the gun, slumped to the floor.

Shoe got to his knees, blood running down his clothes from his shoulder.

"Charlie, call 9-1-1, give my name, a shooting, need an ambulance," Shoe said through his teeth, gripping his arm. "Make it fast."

"Charlie, call 9-1-1," Jeli shouted at him, punching him in the chest to snap him into doing what Shoe said. "I'll get a towel for Shoe's shoulder— stop the bleeding."

"I'll help Billy," Susan said.

Stan was screaming in pain, doubled over his knees.

As Charlie made the 9-1-1 call, he picked up his father's gun, traumatized he pointed the gun at his dad. "You killed grandfather?"

"Charlie, don't," Jeli yelled as she stuffed a towel under Shoe's shirt. "He's not worth killing. Let him rot in jail."

Sirens were heard in the distance, getting louder, louder.

Officers emerged from the staircase, the elevator.

The first officer stepped quickly to Charlie, gently removing the gun from his hand. Another officer picked up the gun lying on the floor next to Billy.

A medic checked Shoe's wound, another checked Wurthy. Another medic knelt by Billy's unconscious body, holding smelling salts reeking of vinegar under his nose. Billy's eyes slowly opened.

Compresses were applied to Wurthy's knee. A medic on either side, they stood him on his feet, marched him to the elevator as he yelled at Charlie. "I'm glad he's dead. Do you hear me, Charlie?

No more blackmail. You and I can go live in a chateau in Italy. It's nice there. I'll see you soon, son," Wurthy said, laughing, his head lolling about.

The elevator door closed.

———

THE MEDI-VAN'S SHRILL siren faded down the street, carrying Stan Wurthy to the hospital in the custody of an officer.

A medic helped Shoe to the elevator at the same time that Officer Stewart hit the stair landing. He took one look at his partner's blood-soaked shirt and pants and told him not to worry, he'd get the status from the officers in the condo and take the statements of the witnesses. "Get yourself patched up, Shoe. I'll brief you after I button up the scene."

The elevator door slid shut.

Officer Stewart turned, entered the condo's blood-spattered living room. He faced four witnesses in shock at what had just transpired.

"Hello, Officer Stewart," Jeli whispered.

"Ms. Bradley," he said, nodding to her.

"You missed it...all the drama," Jeli said, her eyes fixed on the officer, her breathing labored, willing herself to remain standing.

Stewart's eyes roamed around the room—Billy sat on the floor, leaning against the wall by the kitchen island. Charlie was on the couch, Jeli behind him, her hand on his shoulder. Susan stood next to Jeli.

Of the last two officers, one was bagging the guns, shell casings, and blood samples. The other officer was taking pictures—living room, the kitchen island, the front door, and hall to the back door. He took yellow crime-scene tape out of his bag ready to secure the area once everyone left.

Stewart started with Billy. Took his statement, then Charlie's, then Susan's, both saying what they saw, corroborating each other as they had arrived together. None said but a few words, a few words in spurts, then nothing.

It was Susan who said that Jeli saved herself by kneeing Wurthy, also saving Detective Shoe as Wurthy's shot went wide of the detectives head, into his shoulder. At least, that's how she saw it.

Finished with her recollection of the event, Susan asked if she could leave.

Stewart said, yes, but that he may have more questions later.

Susan looked at Jeli, raised her brows—did Jeli want to leave with her? Jeli shook her head-*you go on*.

Billy pulled himself up, clinging to the barstool next to him, clutching the edge of the island. He stood, asked if he could leave. He had Josh Greely's permission to stay in the unit next door for a month until he decided what he was going to do—stay in Boston, or return to Beijing.

From the statements, later to be confirmed with forensics, Stewart learned that Wurthy shot Shoe in the shoulder at the same time Billy shot Wurthy in the knee. Stewart gave Billy permission to leave but reminded him he was still not to leave the city until given clearance by Detective Shoe.

The officers finished gathering evidence.

Jeli slumped on the couch. Charlie remained on the other end slouching, head back.

Jeli stumbled from the couch to the corner in back of the empty wheelchair, crumbling to the floor. Her back against the wall, legs drawn up in the fetal position, her body shaking, convulsing as she gasped for breath, eyes closed. A tear meandered down her cheek. She swiped it away, her arms around her knees.

Officer Stewart approached, squatted in front of her.

"Are you alright, Ms. Bradley?" His voice was soft. He reached for her hand, held tight.

A life line.

Jeli shook her head slowly, once.

Closing her eyes, she breathed deeply, breathed deeply again, her hand gripping his.

"You were very brave," Stewart said.

Jeli began to rock—back and forth, back and forth. She stopped. Sat very still against the wall. Her eyes opened.

"I'm alright," she whispered. "Stay with me a couple of minutes."

"I'll stay as long as you like."

Staring into the officer's eyes, she again breathed deeply, took another deep breath. "Thanks, I'm okay now," she whispered.

"How about a glass of water?" Officer Stewart said.

Jeli nodded, letting go of the officer's hand.

Charlie had raised his head from the back of the couch watching her, watching the officer give her a glass of water.

"Can we go now?" Charlie asked, his voice musky. "I'll see that Anjelica gets home."

"Yes, but I want you both to come to the station or the hospital. I know Detective Shoe will want to talk to you, depending on his injury. He'll call you."

Charlie helped Jeli to her feet. They walked out to the elevator, Charlie's arm around her, supporting her. With a half smile, she said she was fine, and he dropped his arm.

They walked slowly out of the building, sat on the bottom step as Charlie put in a call for an Uber.

"I'll pick you up tomorrow, Anjelica. Let me know what time you want to see the detective."

Jeli nodded that she would call. At the moment, all she wanted to do was go to the apartment, curl up in bed, close her mind from the scene seared into her brain.

Chapter 61

———

THE GRAY BONE-CHILLING day mirrored their mood—somber, portending nothing good from the meeting with Detective Shoe. It had been three days since taking down Stan Wurthy, ending with his arrest.

Shoe entered the precinct conference room—concrete block walls painted puke yellow. Oak conference table, gray metal folding chairs set on gray linoleum tiles with streaks of black and white. Shoe's arm, in a sling, was held close to his body to ease the pain of the shoulder wound. He faced Jeli and Charlie across the table. He sat down, laying a file folder in front of him.

Officer Stewart followed Shoe, nodded to the pair. He set a carafe of coffee, foam cups, and a small dish holding sugar packets and creamers at the end of the table. He then took a seat. He looked at Jeli, raised his brows. She responded with a slight smile—*yes, she was okay.*

"Good morning," Shoe said. "How are you both doing?"

Jeli and Charlie shrugged—as good as could be expected.

"It's a little chilly in here. Help yourself to coffee if you like."

Jeli took him up on the offer. Poured two cups, offering one to Shoe. He accepted and she sat down drawing the dish of sugar, creamers, and stirrers closer. Officer Stewart and Charlie remained seated.

The detective placed a recorder on the table between them. "First thing, we'll go over your statements once again, on the sequence of events that occurred at Mr. Wu's condo, or Mr. Josh Greely's condo to be precise, ending with Stan Wurthy's arrest."

Shoe opened a packet of sugar, shaking it into his coffee. Stewart got up, walked to a small stand, retrieving a fistful of napkins.

Shoe took a sip of coffee. "After that, I'll take you to see your father, Charlie. It's up to you if you want Ms. Bradley to go with you. Okay with both of you?"

Jeli nodded.

Charlie looked at Jeli. "I'd like you to come with me, if you're up to it?"

Jeli nodded again.

Charlie took off his heavy parka, comfortable with a thick, wool turtleneck sweater, jeans, sneakers. Jeli opted to keep her parka on, the toe of her winter boots protruding from under heavy jeans. Her mass of red curls was the only bright spot in the room.

They gave their statements, for the record, prodded by a few questions from Shoe for clarification.

Shoe turned off the recorder.

"Charlie, I don't know how much you've heard about the blackmail letters your grandfather sent to your father. In any event, I have them in this folder. I'd like you to read them before we see your father." Shoe pushed the folder in front of Charlie. He read the first letter twice, shaking his head, looking up at Shoe several times.

Jeli poured herself another cup of coffee.

With a sigh, Charlie closed the folder, sliding the file back to the detective.

"Charlie, your father is being held in the hospital's psychiatric ward. Are you sure you want to see him?"

Charlie balled his fist, then let his hands fall to his side. His body went limp. "So much to absorb, but, yes, I want to see him."

"Officer Stewart, let the hospital know that we are on our way to talk to Stan Wurthy, and that his son will be with us to see his father," Shoe said. "Bring the squad car around. We'll wait for you out front."

————

THE PUNGENT ODOR OF disinfectant swept over the group exiting the elevator at the psychiatric ward. They were met by an orderly who escorted them to a room, so small it could hardly be considered a conference room—rectangular table, three chairs on one side, two on the other.

Jeli stood inside with Officer Stewart at the right of door, both leaning against the wall. Detective Shoe and Charlie sat at the table.

An orderly led Stan Wurthy, handcuffed in front, a large cast on his left leg, foot to thigh, into the cramped space. The officer on duty at the hospital with Wurthy, and the orderly, helped Wurthy sit, his leg stretched out to the side. A grimace of pain crossed Wurthy's face, along with an expletive released silently from his lips.

Wurthy looked up, surprised at seeing Charlie across the table. "Son, this is great. We have to make plans."

"What made you do it?"

"Do what?"

"Kill my grandfather?"

A fog fell over Wurthy's face. "Who are you?"

"I'm your son, Charlie. Why did you kill my grandfather?"

"Kill?'

"Wu Chao."

Wurthy snapped to attention. Spine straight. "Wu Chao, oh yes, I went to see him. We had a terrible argument, really terrible. I had to stop him from saying such vile things, Stan this, Stan that. I had to stop him from blackmailing me. Stop him. Stop him. Oh, yes. I hit him on the head, hit him hard. He fell over, stopped talking, I dragged him to the bedroom but stopped because the foul-mouthed parrot was screeching my name—Stan, Stan, Stan. I stopped it too."

"How did you get in the condo the day you killed my grandfather. The door was locked."

Wurthy's brows scrunched, his head tilting, eyes blank.

"What are you talking about?"

"It's an easy question requiring an easy answer. How did you get in the condo?"

"Oh…oh…your grandfather. Terrible man. He was blackmailing me you know." Wurthy rocked in his chair, peering at Charlie. "Easy question, easy answer. I got the key from your key ring. The pizza was wonderful don't you agree. But Ms. Bradley didn't like it. No, she didn't. I knew she was faking. I saw her holding the emperor, my emperor. I knew right then I had to stop her, stop her for good before she tried to blackmail me." Wurthy hunched over, closed his eyes. "I'm tired, very tired." He tried to stand, cried out in pain.

The orderly and the officer came to his side, helped him up, keeping a firm grip under his arms.

"Very tired," he whispered. "Find us a villa, Charlie, in Italy. You're a good boy. No, you aren't Charlie. Charlie is a baby," he whispered, as he was escorted from the room.

Jeli looked at the floor. There was nowhere else to look. She couldn't bear to look at Charlie. So sad.

Shoe stood up. "Come on, Charlie. I think we're done here."

"Uh, okay."

Officer Stewart held the door for Jeli. Shoe and Charlie followed her out to the hall, followed her out of the hospital into the chill of the gathering clouds.

"Jeli, have a drink with me?" Charlie said quietly, his hand on her arm.

Jeli glanced up at him, nodded.

"Officer Stewart, can you drop us off at the Union Oyster House? I know it's out of your way, but—"

"Not a problem, Charlie."

"Hold up a minute, Charlie," Shoe said. "I have something for you, a copy of Mr. Wu's will. You'll get the original as soon as the investigation is closed. It was at the bottom of the steel case, underneath the folder with the copies of the blackmail letters he sent to your dad." Shoe pulled a folded sheet of paper from the inside pocket of his jacket, handing it to Charlie.

"It's written in his hand, not bad considering English isn't his native language. He leaves everything to you, his grandson. I don't know how much it will amount to—you'll have to figure that out.

The condo is listed. The will is dated the same as the Purchase and Sale agreement. The condo may be a negative. I'm sure Josh Greely will come after you for payment. On the other hand, your grandfather's laundry is under agreement to be sold. I don't know about a mortgage. Anyway, he had a lawyer. His contact information is at the bottom, under the signature."

"Thanks, Detective. I'll definitely follow up."

The ride to the Oyster House was awkward. No one knew what to say, so Charlie, the officer and the detective chose a safe subject—Boston's sports—Red Sox and their coming season, the end of the Patriot's last season.

Jeli didn't join the conversation, letting the men carry the ball. Her thoughts were of the latest turn of events in Charlie's life. She wondered if there might be enough money from his grandfather's laundry to pay for the condo, at least cover the down payment. If he got his act together, went back to work, surely he could handle the mortgage. But would he want to live in a place where his grandfather was killed? After all, he did see his grandfather lying in the doorway to his bedroom. Not an easy image to expunge from his memory.

Looking out the window as Officer Stewart pulled to the curb of the Oyster House, Jeli punched her thigh a couple of good licks—expunging the image of Stan—frail, in-and-out of his right mind. Forcing a smile, to herself only, she was eager to invite Susan to the St. Patrick's Day celebration on the farm next week. *That* was going to be fun!

"I'll get your door, Anjelica," Charlie said, breaking into her thoughts. "Thanks, Officer. You too, Detective. Please keep me posted on the progress of the case."

"I will, Charlie. Goodbye, Ms. Bradley," Shoe said.

Jeli nodded to him, taking Charlie's arm.

The lunch crowd had left, but Charlie asked if they could sit upstairs. The waitress led them to a booth against the wall, and took their drink order, laying the menus on the table.

So, Jeli thought, here we are. I don't know why Charlie asked me to have a drink—romantic, no. Just letting down after a traumatic visit with his dad—could be. What to do with his life—no! She was struggling with that herself.

For once, she didn't start babbling to fill the void, a lull in the conversation. Let him talk first.

"Thanks for coming today, Anjelica. For the most part, Dad seemed a bit crazy, don't you think? He seemed to recall what he did pretty much—striking grandfather on the head, dragging him to the bedroom, killing poor Chang-ying. But then his memory receded. Maybe that's what people do with something so awful. It would haunt anyone."

"The blackmail—your dad must have felt cornered, his business failing and all," Jeli said.

"I suppose so."

The waitress set the drink order on the table—red wine for Jeli, beer on tap for Charlie. Charlie shook his head—nothing more at the moment.

They each took a sip—another lull in the conversation.

"There is one good thing that came out of all this," Charlie said, looking into her eyes.

"What's that?" Jeli said. She caught a look in Charlie's eyes that put her female antennae on alert.

"You."

Oh, dear, no, no. I'm not ready for serious. Maybe I'm wrong, like he wants to be friends. No...he wants more.

"I'm glad we met, too, Charlie. You and Faye Yoon have a lot of catching—"

"Yes, thanks to you. But I was thinking of you and me—after what we went through, to be an *us*. Don't you think?"

Oh God, don't string him along, Anjelica Jane.

"You've been through a lot, Charlie, the past few months—your grandfather, your dad. I've been through a lot, too—launching my interior design business. It's been very exciting. I've met so many new wonderful people—Faye, Susan, you, Josh."

There was a slight uptick of his brows when she mentioned Josh's name. But was it enough to slow him down?

"Your designs for my grandfather were terrific, but...but I guess I never thought you wanted to make a full-time career of it."

"Oh, yes. It's very exciting. Susan and I are going to China for a month. I want to learn more of the culture, establish contacts. Between Quin Shi and Josh, I figure I have a couple of years—all out designing for Josh's renovations, and Shi's China buyers."

"Oh, I see. Do you suppose we could have dinner together...once in awhile."

"Of course. I'd like that. Charlie, I really have to go. I promised Susan I'd be home early. Girl stuff...you know."

"Oh, okay...girl stuff. Well, I have to get going, too. I thought I'd do some fence mending—my old job. I've been hanging out long enough."

"That's a wonderful idea. I'm sure your old boss will be overjoyed to have you back onboard."

"I don't know about overjoyed, but he has called several times."

"See there—we both landed on our feet. It's been a tough year so far, but things are looking up. All we have to do is put one foot in front of the other, our path will become clearer with each step."

"You're right, Anjelica. Thanks again for going to the hospital with me today."

"Always happy to help a friend," Jeli said, with a broad smile.

Charlie offered to see her home, but Jeli wanted to put some distance between them. Giving him a quick peck on the cheek, she strutted off to tackle a list of phantom errands. Breathing a sigh of relief, she stopped at the corner for a stop light. A couple, holding hands, looking adoringly into each other's eyes, stood beside her.

She glanced at the light as it turned green. It's not that I don't want to find somebody. But I'm not going to settle for just any man. Mister Right just hasn't come along yet. I'll know when it happens.

Passing a store, she caught her image in the window. She paused, smiling. Inside she saw a woman, a very pregnant woman. She was talking to a salesclerk about the tiny sleeper set in her hand.

Jeli watched as the clerk handed her a little fuzzy-white teddy bear. The woman wiped a tear away, and grinning, gave the clerk a hug.

Jeli continued to watch. Of course, I want babies...maybe two. They'll love visiting the farm, feeding the chickens, gathering eggs. Children must be part of my life's plan.

Jeli turned away from the window picking up her gait. "First, Jeli-bean, you have to meet Mr. Right...*after* your trip to China."

Epilogue

March 17
St. Patrick's Day

WITH TWO IRISH LASSES in the family, plus a family that never knew a holiday they didn't celebrate, this St. Patty's day looked to go down big in the annuals of the Bradley clan.

Jeli and Susan sauntered down the driveway, a camera swinging from Jeli's hand. Jeli had spoken about her so much, everyone greeted Susan like a long lost member of the family.

The clan was gathering, and Jeli didn't want to miss the chatter she assumed to be about the farm's latest business center—Bradley Farm BrewPub.

Joining her family mingling on the deck, Jeli started lining them up for a family picture. She handed the camera to Susan, designated to be the official photographer of the opening of the pub. Jeli and Finn stood at one end next to Pops, Jane and Gran. Georgie and Wolfe finally emerged all cleaned up from oiling the tractor. Georgie was eager to spread the fertilizer for the coming crop of hops and barley for the brewery.

Katie, Finn's new wife, stepped out the back door of the farmhouse, wiping her hands on her frilly white apron. Daisy, Katie's niece, soon to be adopted by the newlyweds, came running into Finn's arms. Her dog Lucas, the small puff of caramel-colored fur, running beside her as fast as his little legs would go. The second row started with Wolfe and Georgie. Three more were due to arrive shortly.

"Whatta you think, Pops?" Finn said.

"Mighty nice, son. Opening day. It's going to be a great St. Patty's celebration. Your mom and Gran have been cooking for weeks. The freezers are full," Pops said grinning.

Finn saw his partners, Cam and Carrie, Cam's arm about his wife's waist, strolling down the path. Cam, always serious, thinking, thinking over every detail, smiled in spite of himself. Cameron Foster was the real brains behind the enterprise. Finn preferred playing host, marketing to the town, and anyone who stopped to listen to him.

"Hey, Cam, Carrie, come on down, enjoy the view," Finn said pushing his straw cowboy hat up a notch on his brow.

Everyone was lined up with the exception of Marshall, who was picking up Sadie and Travis at Logan Airport. Their estimated time of arrival—any minute.

Everyone turned at the honking of Marshall's Jeep as he drew into the driveway. He pulled up a ways, and parked. The clan broke apart, rushing the arrivals with whoops and hollers, hugs and kisses.

Gran whispered to Jane. "It's going to be a wonderful day, Janie. I can feel it in my bones. The whole family together," she said, pretending there was something in her eye. A tear maybe?

"You're right, Gran. Every one of them."

Jeli once again called for everyone to get ready for the group portrait. This time she lined them up in front of the Bradley Farm sign beside the road. Wolfe had updated the sign, adding a fresh coat of paint to the three shingles swinging in a slight breeze at the bottom of the main sign: Craft Beer, Gift Shop, Herbs and Flowers.

Susan stood her post, took the first picture, showing it to Jeli.

"We have to stand closer together. Sadie, Marsh, Travis, you're the tallest, stand in back. Yep, that looks good. Okay, Susan, try another shot."

Jeli took a look, gave her blessing, and Susan shot three more. Even Lucas sat by Daisy's side dusting the residue of a snow bank with his little tail.

Jeli called to Finn as the line broke up. "What time is the grand opening? I have a ribbon for you and Cam to cut."

"In another hour, two o'clock. Pictures?"

"You got it. Not to worry, Susan and I will set it up. You three open the door and I'll start shooting. Then I think Georgie and Wolfe should stand with you for a few shots. After all, they're plowing the fields of hops and...and whatever," she said grinning.

A florist's van swung into the driveway and stopped. The driver hopped out, smiling from ear to ear. He was one of Finn's schoolmates from high school. "Hey, buddy, I understand there's a new brewpub around here. Seems the whole town's talking about it. Where do you want the flowers—baskets, vases, boxes," he said laughing.

"I'll take care of it, Finn," Carrie said. "Come with me young man. Actually, drive up by the walkway."

"We can help," Sadie and Jeli said.

"Hey don't leave us guys out," Marshall said. "We'll all help."

"Susan, after we take a couple of pics in the pub, let's you and I go up to my room, pick the best, or a couple, and print them for everybody. Okay with you?"

"Sure. Your family is super nice. Do you want me to be a roving photographer when we come down for the opening? I'd like to take the pictures and you'll be busy I'm sure with other stuff—meets and greets of your friends."

"Of course, you're the photographer in-chief, and I want some of you and I together, too. Hey, Georgie, come here a minute."

"What's up? Are you leading your friend—"

"Sort of. When you're done here, can you come up to the house, the attic? I want to scrounge around for some frames. I think when you and I were last in the attic...you know the dresser set—"

"Are you talking about that beautiful green brush and mirror?" Susan asked.

"Sure am. Can you, Georgie?"

"Wouldn't miss it. Give me ten minutes to finish unloading the flowers."

"Come on Susan."

"I'm with you."

"By the way, I don't think I told you about Billy Qiáng."

"The big man who took care of Mr. Wu?" Susan said.

"That's the one. Well, I was talking to Faye Yoon and one thing led to another. The upshot...Billy is going to work for her. It's super cool because he speaks Chinese and with her clientele...well, you catch my drift."

"What about Charlie? Do you think you did the right thing...literally cutting the guy loose?"

"Susan, you make me sound heartless."

"Just sayin."

"I didn't want to string him along, when in my heart of hearts he wasn't *the one.* An occasional dinner is one thing, a full-out commitment another. Besides, there is something I just found out before you and I caught the train to come to the farm. Faye called. She actually sounded excited. Charlie is taking possession of the condo his grandfather left to him in his will. Faye says he has the money for a down payment and his grandfather's lawyer told him there could be upwards of $100,000 once all is said and done. Best of all, Charlie is back at work."

"I'm happy to hear things are working out for him. He certainly had more than one gut punch the last two months."

The girls paused at the top of the driveway, looking over the fields, down to the road, the barn now a brewpub.

"Jeli, I hope I'm not putting your mom out. I love my room...she made up the bed for me, towels, some wonderful soap...lavender I think."

"Not to worry. She loves it. I'm sure the soap is one that Katie made. She and Carrie are trying to beef up the gift center, but they have their plates full with the brewpub. Okay, let's load the pictures on my computer. Georgie should be here any minute. Depending on the size frame, I could send the picture we like the best to the printer in town. We could pick it up, hang it in the pub before everyone leaves."

"Jeli...the attic? You told me about a ghost, maybe the one who used the dresser set you found. Do you think we'll see her?"

"Oh, I've never seen her...you'll just know she's there, and—"

"Hey, I'm here. You girls ready to look for some frames?" Georgie said, puffing from his dash up the driveway.

"Yes, and Susan wants to see Rosemary. I said we've never seen her...only felt her presence...you and me."

"Well, there's always a first time. Let's go...wooohooo," Georgie said, flashing googly eyes at the girls.

The attic was bone-chilling cold, a ray of sun cutting a swath of light across the creaky floorboards.

"Where did we see the frames, Georgie?" Jeli said.

"I think it was in the far corner."

Jeli tiptoed along the sunbeam, "There, I see a couple...oh, there's a good-sized one—sixteen inches wide, I'd guess." Jeli stooped over, picked up the frame as Georgie crept in behind her, running his fingertips up her arm.

Jeli screamed, whirling around, hands on her hips. "Georgie...Georgie don't ever do that again. You scared me," Jeli said struggling to catch her breath.

Georgie chuckled. "Sorry."

"It's not funny—"

"I agree," Susan said. "If you found what you want let's get out of here."

"Wait, did you feel that?" Jeli said.

Jeli gently rubbed her arm as did Georgie.

"This is the one. This is it," Jeli said, tracing the top of the frame with her finger.

"What makes you so sure?" Susan said, rubbing her own arm.

"Rosemary's here. She wants me to take this frame."

"I agree," Georgie said. "It looks like it needs a bit of tender loving care though. I can fix it, clean it up."

"That would be great. Change of plans. It doesn't have to be ready today. I'll take the frame back to Boston with me and have a print shop frame the picture up, plus a mat. I can bring everything back with me on Mom's birthday, April fifteenth."

"You guys are nuts. Can we leave now?" Susan said.

Jeli smiled, giving Georgie a hug. "You're not forgiven totally…maybe a little, but don't scare me again. Understood?"

"Yes, ma'am. Understood," Georgie said, grinning as he grasped the frame from her fingers.

———

A LITTLE BEFORE TWO O'CLOCK, the clan gathered on the barn's deck in front of the main entrance to the brewpub. Jeli positioned Carrie at one end of a wide burnished gold ribbon, and Katie held the other spanning the width of the door. Jeli had snagged Gran's oversized sewing scissors she once used to cut fabric. She handed the scissors to Finn. Cam put his fingers over Finn's.

The moment had arrived.

Their dreams becoming reality.

Susan yelled, "Say cheese."

The partners cut the ribbon to the cheers of the Bradley clan and about a dozen eager beavers who came to be in on the opening of Lakeville's first brewery.

Jeli and Sadie told Gran and their mom to sit and enjoy the celebration. "We girls will put out the food you've been slaving over."

"The corned beef and cabbage needs to be sliced, Sadie," Gran said.

"And Carrie is baking the cornbread back in the pub's kitchen. Let us know if she needs help," Jane said.

"We will. Sit. Enjoy. Finn, can you serve up a glass of beer from your inaugural keg to Mom and Gran?" Jeli said.

"Coming right up. I see Pops. I'll get a glass for him, too...and Wolfe and Georgie...and you girls."

Wolfe and Georgie sidled up to the table, everyone raising their glasses to Finn. While Jeli had them corralled, and with Susan by her side capturing the moment with her camera, Jeli sprang her big news.

"I'm going to China with Susan...in June...for a month."

No one said a word. They were stunned. Anjelica Jane, the baby, was going to China?

Jeli and Susan beamed at each other, as the family sat around the table staring at them.

"Say something...like great...wonderful...have a good trip," Jeli said.

"Yes, great...everything you ticked off," Pops said.

"Susan, do you think it's wise?" Jane said.

"I think it's wonderful, and don't worry, most of the time we'll stay with my family in Beijing."

"Oh well, that's better," Gran said.

Laughter, chatter suddenly broke out at the front door. A group of Finn's friends were congratulating him. Finn called Cameron over, introducing the brew master to their guests.

Finn and Cameron had decided that happy hour would be from two to three—everything free. From then on the customers would be charged for the beer, but not the food. They'd serve the typical Irish fare until it ran out.

Wolfe and Georgie were taking turns manning the cash register, Daisy was charged with making sure the pretzel bowls remained full, and Katie donned her waitress costume—frilly apron over a white blouse, black skirt, and comfy black sneakers. Carrie helped with the beer orders in-between making sure she kept up with the cornbread. They'd also arranged for part-time help in the pub. New hires would start their jobs at eight o'clock until closing.

The barn, after a massive renovation, transformed to a brewpub, came to life with tiny twinkling white lights strung along the bottom of the hayloft. The wall behind the semi-circular bar featured the brew taps, each connected to a large keg on the other side of the wall, ready to be served to the new patrons. Booths were built around the perimeter, tables and chairs set in the expansive central area, as well as in the loft. Katie, Carrie and Daisy had worked long into the night attaching green and white streamers from the wagon wheel fixtures hanging from the ceiling to the wooden slat rails along the loft. Each table had a votive candle flickering inside a frosted glass holder.

With the continuing commotion, townies dropping in to sample the new brews, Sadie poured a beer with a nice head of foam for herself and her twin. She caught him leaning against the wall with his cell to his ear. He rang off as Sadie handed him the beer.

"Here's to you, little brother, safe and sound back in the States."

Marshall raised his glass to her with a smile. "I'm scheduled to return to Tel-Aviv next week. I wasn't going to tell Mom and Pops. You know how they worry. After that terrorist attack last November in Paris, they don't like any of us going out of the country."

"Umm, no grousing over my calling you little brother—"

"Twenty minutes doesn't make me a little brother."

"Umm hmm. Me thinks there is something more in Tel-Aviv besides company business...a little funny business?"

Marshall blew out a puff of air. "Maybe."

"Ahh. Is she Israeli?"

"Yes, if you must know...and no more questions."

"Hey, Sadie," Finn called out. "I changed into my sequin jeans, shirt. How about joining me. These folks are clamoring for us to start strumming a little dance music."

"I'll be right with you, Finn. Do you have my guitar?"

"Right here."

Sadie kissed Marshall's check. "Keep me posted...when you feel like talking about things business related. Funny business, that is."

Sadie hitched up on a stool next to Finn, grabbing her guitar he held out to her. They strummed a few cords, then slammed into a barn-burning country western song.

The barn began to rock, and rock, and rock some more.

It was a good time in Lakeville's newest business.

Katie came around, refreshed everyone's glasses as patrons sang, stomped their feet to the beat.

Jane looked at Gran, tilted her head at the door. Gran nodded. It was time for their version of girl talk.

———

BREATHING IN THE FRESH, crisp night air, they settled in the Adirondack chairs on the deck. In tandem, the two ladies reached in their coat pockets for their packet of cigarillos. Jane flipped her lighter to the tip of Gran's lady's cigar, and then lit her own. They leaned back looking up at the stars, enjoying the night.

Tiny white lights outlined the roof of the barn—the windows, the railing around the deck. Two spotlights attached to the eves, illuminated the words painted on the roof: Bradley Farm BrewPub.

"They're all grown up...how many more coming do you think? Did you know that Carrie is pregnant?" Jane said, releasing a puff of smoke in a perfect "O".

"I guessed it," Gran said.

Jane giggled. "You knew I was pregnant before I did. Just imagine...our Anjelica Jane going to China. She seems to have launched a solid new career at last. The two men she mentioned the last visit no longer seem to be in the picture. I gather there's no time for a serious relationship at the moment. Not ready to settle down or commit. Happy playing the field, I guess. She loves being a mover and a shaker," Jane said.

"Only Marshall and Georgie left to find someone," Gran said, releasing a small puff of smoke. "Look at that moon, Janie. I think I can reach up and touch it," Gran said.

"Do you feel as content as I do tonight?" Jane said.

"Glad you added tonight. Yes, but a new dawn has a way of turning our world upside down," Gran said.

"I know...but still, tonight is to be savored," Jane said. "Tomorrow will come soon enough."

The End

Author's Note

Jeli seems to have settled on an exciting path to her future in interior design. It fits her.

Of course, the question remains: who is Rosemary? Jeli, Wolfe, and Susan certainly felt her presence in the attic of the farmhouse, but still no resolution.

— — —

Marshall, Bradley Farm Series, Book 5
Marshall is on his way again to Tel-Aviv. He tells his family that it's business. Personally I think it's more than business. We'll see.

Acknowledgements

The Guardian, British national daily newspaper articles on the 2015/2016 Chinese Stock Market Crash.

It's All Chinese to Me, An Overview of Culture and Etiquette in China, Pierre Ostrowski & Gwen Penner, Tuttle Publishing, 2009

Kudos, as always, to my reviewers for their unique perspectives on the big picture, digging deep for meaning and structure:
Molly Tredwell, Peggy Keeney, Geri Rogers, Roger and Pat Grady.

About the Author

Life tests us every day, so when we find a precious moment of pleasure, it is to be enjoyed. Such is my new, previously loved car. Her name is Sadie, because as a writer I name everything, of course.

Maybe she'll be decked out by the end of the next book, Book 5, in the Bradley Farm series. I'm thinking a quill pen writing:

MaryJaneForbes.com
cozy, romantic mysteries

NEXT BOOK IN SERIES
Marshall, Bradley Farm Series Book 5

He tracks down cyber criminals. She trains Israeli soldiers. Can their love survive a global conspiracy?

Marshall Bradley's business is on the cutting edge of cyber security. So when a top Israeli tech expert wants to team up on an innovative defense system, he jumps on the first plane to Tel-Aviv. After his stressful days at the office, he escapes into the city's vibrant nightlife... and loses his heart to a ballad singer who's as dangerous as she is beautiful.

Enchanted by the Army weapons trainer with an angel's voice, he walks hand-in-hand with Anna Goldman through the breathtaking historic sites and charming streets of her homeland. But his courtship of Anna and her Israeli lifestyle hits a reality check when sirens fill the air and a cyber breach threatens to weaponize international secrets.

With danger lurking around every corner, can Marshall unmask a hacker with the power to destroy his new love and stir up a fresh wave of bloody chaos?

Marshall is the fifth standalone novel in the captivating Bradley Farm romantic mystery saga. If you like global conspiracies, tech-savvy suspense, and vivid cultural backdrops, then you'll love Mary Jane Forbes' explosive love story.

BRADLEY FARM SERIES

www.ingramcontent.com/pod-product-compliance
Lightning Source LLC
Chambersburg PA
CBHW070608130626
46556CB00001B/305